THE NEW EPICUREAN
&
THE YELLOW ROOM

THE NEW EPICUREAN

&

THE YELLOW ROOM

WORDSWORTH CLASSICS

The paper in this book is produced from pure wood
pulp, without the use of chlorine or any other substance
harmful to the environment. The energy used in its
production consists almost entirely of hydroelectricity
and heat generated from waste material, thereby
conserving fossil fuels and contributing little to the
greenhouse effect.

This edition published 1995 by
Wordsworth Editions Limited
Cumberland House, Crib Street
Ware, Hertfordshire SG12 9ET

ISBN 1 85326 605 1

Typeset in the UK by Antony Gray
Printed and bound in Denmark by Nørhaven

Contents

THE NEW EPICUREAN

Gentle Reader. . .	9
To Lesbia	12
To Lais	16
To Sappho	20
To Julia	28
To Euphrosyne	33
To Lais	42
To Thalia	44
To Helen	50
To Livia	53
To Thalia	61
Conclusion: To Thalia	67

THE YELLOW ROOM

ONE	*Simply Shocked*	71
TWO	*Initiation*	82
THREE	*Mystery*	97
FOUR	*Mystery Unveiled*	106
FIVE	*Punishment*	119
SIX	*The End*	126

THE NEW EPICUREAN

Gentle Reader . . .

Before transcribing my correspondence with my fair friends, it is necessary to describe the scene of the amours alluded to in the letters, and also to say a few words regarding the chief actor, myself.

I am a man who, having passed the Rubicon of youth, has arrived at that age when the passions require a more stimulating diet than is to be found in the arms of every painted courtesan.

That I might the better carry out my philosophical design of pleasure without riot and refined voluptuous enjoyment without alloy, and with safety, I became the purchaser of a suburban villa situated in extensive grounds, embosomed in lofty trees, and surrounded with high walls. This villa I altered to suit my taste and had it so contrived that all the windows faced towards the road, except the French ones, which opened on the lawn from a charming room, to which I had ingress from the grounds at the back and which was quite cut off from the rest of the house. To render these grounds more private, high walls extended like wings from either side of the house and joined the outer walls. I thus secured an area of some five acres of woodland which was not overlooked from any quarter, and where everything that took place would be a secret unknown to the servants in the villa.

The grounds I had laid out in the true English style, with umbrageous walks, alcoves, grottoes, fountains, and every adjunct that could add to their rustic beauty. In the open space, facing the secret apartment before alluded to, was spread out a fine lawn, embossed with beds of the choicest flowers, and in the centre, from a bouquet of maiden's blush roses, appeared a statue of Venus; in white marble at the end of every shady valley was a terminal figure of the god of gardens in his various forms: either bearded like the antique head of the Indian Bacchus; soft and feminine, as we see the lovely Antinous; or Hermaphroditic – the form of a lovely girl with puerile attributes. In the fountains swam gold and silver fish, whilst rare crystals and spars glittered amidst mother o' pearl at the bottom of the basins.

The gardeners who kept this happy valley in order were only admitted on Mondays and Tuesdays, which days were devoted by me entirely to study, the remaining four being sacred to Venus and love.

This garden had three massive doors in its walls, each fitted with a small lock made for the purpose, and all opened with a gold key which never left my watch guard.

Such were the external arrangements of my Caproe. Now, a few words on the internal economy of my private *salle d'amour* and I have done.

This apartment, which was large and lofty, was in its fittings and furniture entirely Louis-Quinze, that is to say, in the latest French mode; the walls were panelled and painted in pale French grey, white and gold, and were rendered less formal by being hung with exquisite paintings by Watteau. Cabinets of buhl and marqueterie lined the sides, each filled with erotic works by the best authors, illustrated with exquisite and exciting prints and charmingly bound. The couches and chairs were of ormolu, covered *en suite* with grey satin, and stuffed with down. The legs of the tables were also gilt, the tops were slabs of marble, which, when not in use for the delicious collations (which were from time to time served up through a trap door in the floor), were covered with rich tapestries. The window curtains were of grey silk and Venetian blinds, painted a pale rose colour, cast a voluptuous shade over the room.

The chimney-piece was of marble, large, lofty, and covered with sculpture in relief, representing beautiful naked children of both sexes in every wanton attitude, entwined with grapes and flowers, carved by the hand of a master. The sides and hearth of this elegant fireplace were encrusted with porcelain tiles of rare beauty, representing the Triumph of Venus, and silver dogs were placed on either side to support the wood, according to the style in vogue in the middle of the last century.

To complete the *coup d'œil*, my embroidered suit of garnet velvet, plumed hat, and diamond hilted sword were carelessly flung upon a chair, while the cabinets and sideboards were covered with costly snuff boxes and china. Such were some of the striking features of this delightful chamber. As for the rest of the house, it was furnished like any other respectable domicile of our times.

My establishment consisted of a discreet old housekeeper, who was well paid and not too sharply looked after in the little matters of perquisites and peculations, a bouncing blooming cook and a sprightly trim housemaid, who were kept in good humour by an occasional half-guinea, a holiday, and a chuck under the chin. Beyond these innocent liberties they were not molested. As for the gardeners, they lived out of the house, and being as well paid for their two days' work as if they worked all the week, it followed that they knew their own interests too well to manifest any undue or indiscreet curiosity as to what passed in the grounds when their services were not required.

Having thus given a sketch of the premises, I proceed at once with the letters, only expressing a hope that you, most courteous reader, will quietly lay down the book if it is too strong for your stomach instead of falling foul of

Your humble servant

THE AUTHOR

To Lesbia

You ask me, most charming Lesbia, to relieve the ennui which your too venerable and too watchful lord causes you to suffer, with his officious attentions, by a recital of some of those scenes which are not visible to the uninitiated; and I, having always been your slave, hasten to obey.

You must know then, *chère petite*, that I have certain convenient ladies in my pay, whom I call pointers, forasmuch as they put up the game.

Last Thursday as I lay stretched on a sofa absorbed in that most charming of Diderot's works *La Religieuse*, the silver bell which communicates with the southern gate gave tongue and roused me from my lethargy. I sprang to my feet and wending my way through that avenue of chestnut trees, which you and I, Lesbia, know so well, made direct for the gate. Here the well-known chariot met my eye, and it only required a glance at the smart coachman to show me that Jehu was none other than Madame R herself; and a devilish handsome groom she made, I can assure you.

An almost imperceptible raising of the eyebrows and a gesture with her whip handle towards the interior of the carriage told me all I wanted to know; so first looking up and down the road to see that we were not observed, I whispered, 'ten o'clock' and then opened the door. 'Come my little darlings,' said I to two delicious young creatures, who, coquettishly dressed with the most charming little hats in the world and full petticoats that barely reached their rose coloured garters, sprang, nothing loth, into my arms. The next minute we were all three standing in the garden, the door was locked, and the chariot had driven off. The elder of my little pets was a blooming blonde, with soft brown hair that shone like gold, melting eyes of the loveliest blue, and cheeks tinted with the softest blush of the rose; a pert little nose slightly *retroussé*, carmine lips, and teeth like pearls completed a most delicious face. She was, she said, just thirteen years old. Her companion, a sparkling brunette with dark eyes, raven hair, and a colour that vied with the damask rose, was about twelve. They were charming children, and when I tell you that their limbs were moulded in the most perfect symmetry and that their manners were cultivated, elegant, and gay, I think you will agree with me that Madame R had catered well.

'Now my little loves,' said I, giving each a kiss, 'what shall we do first; are you hungry, will you eat?'

This proposal seemed to give great satisfaction, so taking each by the hand I led them to my room; and patties, strawberries and cream, apricots, and champagne disappeared with incredible rapidity. While they were eating, I was exploring; now patting the firm dimpled peach-like bottom of the pretty brunette, now inserting a finger into the pouting hairless cleft of the lovely blonde. The latter was called Blanche and the former Cerise. I was beside myself with rapture, and turning first to one and then to the other, covered them with kisses. The collation finished at last, we all went into the grounds, and having walked them round and shown them everything curious, not forgetting the statue of that most impudent god Priapus, at whose grotesque appearance, with his great prick sticking out, they laughed heartily, I proposed to give them a swing. Of course in putting them in I took care that their lovely little posteriors should bulge out beyond the velvet seat, and as their clothes were short, every time they swung high in the air I had a full expansive view of those white globes, and the tempting rose coloured slits that pouted between them; then, oh! the dear little feet, the fucktious shoes, the racy delectable legs; nothing could be finer. But the sight was too tantalising. We were all heated; I with the exertion of swinging them, they with the wine, so they readily agreed to my proposal to proceed to a retired spot, where was a little lake lined with marble, not more than four feet deep. We were soon naked and sporting in the water; then only was it that I could take in all their loveliness at a glance. The budding small pointed breasts, just beginning to grow; the polished ivory shoulders, the exquisite fall in the back, the tiny waist, the bulging voluptuous hips, the dimpled bottoms, blushing and fresh, the plump thighs and smooth white bellies. In a moment my truncheon stood up hard and firm as a constable's staff. I put it in their hands, I frigged and kissed their fragrant cunnies, I gamahuched them, and then the saucy Cerise, taking my ruby-tipped ferrule in her little rosy mouth, began rolling her tongue round it in such a way that I nearly fainted with bliss. At that moment our position was this: I lay stretched on my back on the grass; Blanche sat over me, a leg on either side, with my tongue glued

to her rose. Cerise knelt astride of me also, with her posteriors well
jutted out towards me, and one of my fingers was inserted in her
rosebud. Nor were the hands of the delicious brunette idle: with her
right she played with my balls and with the forefinger of her left hand
she exquisitely titillated the regions beneath. But human nature could
not stand this long; so changing our position I placed Blanche on her
hands and knees while Cerise inserted my arrow, covered with saliva
from her mouth, into the pretty Blanche. She was tight, but not a
virgin, so after a thrust or two I fairly went in up to the hilt. All this
while Cerise was tickling me and rubbing her beautiful body against
me. Soon Blanche began to spend, and to sigh out, 'Oh! oh! dear sir,
give it me now! Shoot it into me! Ah! I faint! I die!' and as the warm
fluid gushed into her she fell prone on the ground.

When Blanche had a little recovered herself we again plunged into
the lake to wash off the dew of love with which we were drenched.

Thus sporting in the water, toying with each other, we whiled away
the hours of the afternoon, till tired, at length, we left the lake and
dressed ourselves. The sun had long disappeared behind the trees and
the shades of evening began to close in. I therefore proposed to adjourn
to the villa, where for some time I amused my little friends with bawdy
books and prints. But you are not to suppose that my hands were idle,
one being under the clothes of each.

Cerise had thrust her hand into my breeches and was manipulating
with great industry, which amused me very much; but I soon found out
the reason, for presently she said, pouting out her pretty mouth, 'You
like Blanche better than me!'

'I love you both, my angels,' said I, laughing heartily at the little
puss's jealousy.

'Ah, it's all very well to laugh,' cried Cerise, 'but I don't see why I am
not to be fucked as well as her!'

'Oh!' I exclaimed, 'that's the way the wind blows, is it!' And drawing
the sweet girl to a couch I tossed up her clothes in a moment.

'Quick, quick, Blanche!' cried Cerise, 'come and gamahuche the
gentleman and make his yard measure stiff before he begins, for you
know how tight I am at first.'

The little Blanche flung down the book she was looking at, and
running up to me placed herself on her knees; then clasping my naked
thighs with her milky arms she seized upon the red head of my thyrsus
and worked her mouth up and down upon it in the most luscious
manner possible. In a few minutes more I could certainly have spent on
her tongue had not Cerise, fearful of being baulked, made her leave off.

Then guiding the randy prick into her opening rosy little cunny, she began to bound and wriggle and twist until she had worked it well in; then twining her legs around my loins and thrusting her tongue in my mouth she gave way unrestrained to the joys of sensation. I was astonished that so young a creature could be so precocious, but I learnt from Madame R, who had brought her up, that every pain had been taken to excite these passions in this girl since she was seven years of age; first with boys, and subsequently with grown-up persons. Blanche I had thought most delicious, but there was a furore in Cerise's fucking which carried you away, as it were, out of yourself.

So great was the delight I experienced with this amorous girl, that I held back as long as possible but she bounded about with such energy that she soon brought down another shower of dew, and all was over. I was glad to hide the diminished head of poor Pego in my white silk breeches, and it being now nearly ten o'clock I rang for chocolate, which soon appeared through the trap door, served up in pretty little porcelain cups with ratafia cakes and bonbons, to which the girls did ample justice. The bell having announced Madame R at the gate, we went forth hand in hand, I having first placed in their pockets a bright new guinea apiece.

Arrived at the gate, I gave her ladyship a pocket-book containing twenty pounds, with which she seemed well content.

'Adieu, my dear children,' said I; 'I hope before long you will pay me another visit.'

'Goodbye, sir,' cried both the girls in a breath, and the chariot drove off.

Quite tired by this time, I locked the gate, and going round to the front of the villa I knocked and entered, as if I had just come home, retiring soon after to bed to dream over again of the joys of that delightful evening.

To Lais

I am afraid, my pretty Lais, I am in disgrace with you for not writing before, so to excuse my seeming neglect, I will now narrate to you an adventure I have lately had here which will amuse you very much. You may remember, possibly, pretty Mrs H, the wife of an old prig of a grocer, whom you met here once. Well, she came to see me the other day and, after I had done justice to her charms, which indeed are not to be despised, sitting on my knee and sipping some old Burgundy, for which the fine dame has a great liking, she told me the cause of her visit.

'As you are so generous,' she began, 'it always gives me great pleasure to oblige you and throw anything in your way that is worthy of the notice of such a true Epicurean. Now I have just received from the country a niece whose father has been long dead and who has now lost her mother, so the good people of the place where they lived, to get rid of the orphan, have sent her up to me. This has vexed my good man not a little – as you know he loves his money dearly; not able to get a child for himself, he has no fancy to be saddled with other people's. But I quieted him with the assurance that I would get her a place in a few days. The girl is just seventeen, as beautiful and fresh as an angel and innocent as a baby, so I thought what a nice amusement it would be for you to have her here and enlighten and instruct her. You have, I know, a little cottage fitted up as a dairy; engage her as your dairymaid, buy a cow or two, and the thing is done.'

'But,' said I, 'won't she be afraid to live in the cottage all alone, and if the gardeners should find it out what would they think!'

'Nay, sir,' said the tempter, 'your honour knows best, but it seems to me that these difficulties can easily be got over. I know an old crone, a simple, poor, humble creature, who would do anything for half a crown and be delighted to live in that cottage. She alone will be seen by the gardeners, and my niece will be kept close during the two days they work in the grounds.'

'That will do capitally,' said I. 'You arrange it all.'

Accordingly, old mother Jukes and the blooming Phoebe were duly installed. Two Alderney cows occupied the cowhouse and the new dairymaid set to work. After two or three days had passed, I went one afternoon to see her milk the cows. She jumped up from her three-legged stool in confusion, and blushing deeply, dropped me a rustic curtsey.

'Well, Phoebe,' said I gently, 'what do you think of the dairy? Do you think you shall like the place?'

She dropped me another curtsey, and replied, 'Yes, an't please ye, sir.'

'You find the cottage convenient?' said I.

'Oh la! sir, mighty,' cried Phoebe.

'Very good,' said I, 'now when you have done milking, I will show you the poultry yard and my pet animals, all of which are to be under your care.'

As soon as the fair creature had drawn off as much milk as she required, she placed her pails in the dairy and, smoothing down her white apron, attended me. We went first to the poultry yard, where Phoebe espied the cock treading one of the hens.

'Oh, my,' she exclaimed, 'that cruel cock; look at him, a-pecking and trampling upon that poor hen. That is just the way they used to go on at feyther's, but I won't let un do it.' And she ran forward to drive away the cock.

'Stop, stop, Phoebe,' I exclaimed; 'do not drive him away, for if the cock does not tread the hen, how are we to have any chickens?'

'Sure, sir, the chickens will come from the eggs, and if he treads upon the poor hen that way, he will break them all in her belly, other while.'

'Not at all,' said I. 'It is true pullets lay eggs, and very good are such eggs for eating, but they will never come to chickens. It is the cocks who make the chickens.'

Phoebe opened her large blue eyes very wide at this, and ejaculated, 'Mighty!'

'Don't you see, Phoebe, that while he is treading, he is also doing something else?'

'Noa, sir, I doant,' said Phoebe demurely.

'If you look at the hen's tail, Phoebe, you will see that it is lifted up and spread open; there, now look; and you will see the cock is putting something in the opening under her tail.'

'Oh, la, yes,' cried she, blushing as red as a peony; 'I see now, well I never.'

'You see, Phoebe, you have much to learn; but come to the stable and I will show you something more extraordinary. Where, may I ask, do you suppose foals come from? And kittens, and puppies?'

'Lawk sir, from their mothers, I suppose.'

'Yes, but they would not come without they were made; now you shall see what my little stallion pony will do when I let him into the stall of the mare, and some months hence you shall see the foal he has made.'

To this Phoebe could only respond, 'Mighty!'

We went to the stable. The ponies were beautiful little creatures, of a fine cream colour, and pure Pegu breed, sent to me from Burma by a friend.

Like all horses of that colour, their noses, pizzle, etc., were flesh colour, and therefore at once caught the eye. Removing the bar that divided the loose box, I let the stallion pass into the other side. The little mare received him with a neigh of welcome.

'Oh, my,' cried Phoebe, 'she seems to know him quite nat'ral loike.'

The stallion began nibbling at different parts of the mare, who raised her tail, and again neighed. Her lover answered the neigh. Soon he began to scent her sexual beauties, which he caressed with his lips, his enormous yard shot out and banged against his stifle. I pointed it out to Phoebe.

'Oh, good lud! yes, sir, I sees it!' cried she, blushing up very red and trembling all over.

I passed my arm round her taper waist and, gently kissing her, whispered, 'Now observe what he will do.'

Presently the stallion mounted on his hind legs, embracing the mare with the fore ones, and his great pizzle began to enter; the mare stood firm and did not kick. He laid his head along her back, nibbling her coat. He moved backwards and forwards. Phoebe trembled and turned red and pale by turns. The mare whinnied with delight, the stallion responded.

'See, Phoebe,' said I, 'how these lovers enjoy themselves. Mon Dieu! how happy they are!'

'La, sir,' cried the girl, 'what pleasure can she take in having that great long thing put into her body?'

'The pleasure,' said I sententiously, 'which nature gives to those who propagate their kind; and some day my little Phoebe will feel the same pleasure. But look! He has finished, and is out again. See how the female parts of the mare open and shut with spasms of delight.

Observe how she cocks her tail – see how she turns her head, as if asking for more. There now, she neighs again.'

But Phoebe was not listening; she had seated herself on a truss of hay, and with her eyes fixed on the again stiffening pizzle of the stallion had fallen into a reverie. I guessed what she was thinking about, so seating myself by her side I stole a hand up her clothes. She trembled, but did not resist. I felt her firm plump thighs, I explored higher – I touched her feather: soft and silky as a mouse's skin was the moss in which I entwined my fingers. I opened the lips, heavens! could I believe my senses. She was spending and her shift was quite wet. Whether it was accident or not I cannot say, but she had dropped one of her hands on my lap.

My truncheon had long been stiff as iron; this additional aggravation had such an effect that, with a start, away flew too material buttons and Jack sprang out of his box into her hand. At this she gave a little scream, and snatching away her own hand, at the same time pushed away mine. Jumping up, she began smoothing down her rumpled clothes and with great vehemence exclaimed, 'Oh, la! fie, sir: doantee, doantee. Oh, I'm afeard,' etc., etc.

But I was not going to lose such a chance and began to soothe her with talk, until at length we got back to the same position again. I grew more bold, I kissed her eyes and her bosom; I handled her lovely buttocks; I frigged her clitoris – her eyes sparkled; she seized upon that weapon which had at first so frightened her, and the next minute I had flung her back on the hay and was frigging away at her maidenhead; but she made a terrible outcry and struggled most violently. Fortunately, Mrs Jukes had a convenient attack of deafness, and heard nothing, so that after a good deal of trouble I found myself in possession of the fortress, up to the hilt. Once in, I knew well how to plant my touches, and ere long a soft languor pervaded all her limbs, pleasure succeeded pain. She no longer repulsed me but, sobbing on my shoulder, stopped now and then to kiss my cheek.

Her climax came at length and then she threw all modesty aside, entwined her lovely legs around my back, twisted, wriggled, bit, pinched and, kissing me with ardour, seemed to wake up to the new life she had found.

Thrice we renewed the seraphic joys; and then and not till then did I leave her to her poultry yard and her dairy.

She is still with me; an adept in the wiles of love; not the least jealous, but very useful to me in all the other little affairs which I have on hand. As for Mrs H, I gave her fifty guineas for her niece's maidenhead; and although I have bought many much dearer, I never enjoyed it as I did with Phoebe.

So now good-night, and if you can sleep without a lover after such a recital, it is more than I can; so I shall seek the arms of this unsophisticated country lass to allay the fires that recording this narrative has lit up in my veins.

To Sappho

You complain, my sweet girl, that it is long since you heard from me, and remind me that I, of all men, am the only one who could ever give you delight. In reply to your complaint, I must assure you that had there been anything to relate which would have been likely to interest my young philosopher I should have written, but I know too well that ordinary love affairs between men and women do not much amuse you and that the loves of girls for each other are more to your taste. By your other remark I am much flattered; and if you can frame some excuse to your aunt for leaving home and will come here, I think I can show you how to pass an agreeable afternoon. In the interim I will detail an adventure which I met with the other day, and I think will vastly please your fancy.

I was strolling out in one of those thick woods which abound in this neighbourhood when in a secluded dell I espied two young ladies seated very lovingly together, engaged in earnest conversation. They were so absorbed in their discourse that I found no difficulty in approaching softly to within a yard of the spot and, concealing myself in a thicket, I sat down on the turf to listen to them.

The elder of the two was a fine handsome woman of about five or six and twenty, with lustrous dark eyes, black hair, an aquiline nose, and noble figure, yet rather too masculine looking to be altogether pleasing. Her companion was a lovely girl of sixteen, a most exquisite face of a perfect oval, laughing blue eyes shaded with long black lashes, and a profusion of the most beautiful hair of a light auburn which wantoned in the breeze in a hundred lovelocks, forming a most charming picture; her figure was exquisitely rounded in all the witchery of early girlhood, and its undulations raised certain strong desires in my heart to be better acquainted with its beauties.

I now set myself to listen to their conversation.

'I assure you,' the dark-eyed woman was saying, 'there is nothing in it; these men are the most selfish creatures in the world; and besides, what pleasure, think you, can they give us that we do not have already without their aid?'

'Well, dear friend,' laughed the girl, in a sweet silvery voice, 'I am sure you talk very sensibly, but yet there must be something in the joys of love, if we are to believe the poets, who have so often made it their theme; besides, I do not mind telling you that I know a little more about the subject than you may suppose.'

'Mon Dieu,' ejaculated the dark beauty, who I now began to think was a Frenchwoman, especially as I had already noticed a slight foreign accent in her voice; 'Mon Dieu' (and she turned pale), 'how is it possible you should know anything of love at your age?'

'Shall I tell you?' replied the young girl.

'Ah! yes, yes; tell me, *ma chère*.'

'Well then, dear; you know young Mrs Leslie?'

'Certainly.'

'She was a former school-fellow of mine; and a month or two after her honeymoon, I went on a visit to that pretty country seat of her husband's, Harpsdeen Court, in Bedfordshire. While there she not only told me all about the secret joys of matrimony, but permitted me to witness her bliss.'

'To witness it? Incredible!'

''Tis a fact, I do assure you; shall I tell you what I saw, and how I saw it?'

'Oh yes, *ma petite*, I do not mind what you may have seen, I was only afraid one of these perfidious men had captivated your poor little heart; as it was a mere girlish frolic, it will amuse me very much to hear all about it.'

The young girl, first giving her friend a sweet kiss, which I envied, thus began:

'My friend Clara Leslie, though she has a pleasing amiable face, is not strictly handsome, but nature, you know, is full of compensations, as her husband found out to his great satisfaction. She has a shape that vies with the Venus de Medici, the most lovely figure you ever beheld.

When quite a girl at school, she could show a leg that any woman might envy, but now at twenty years of age she surpassed the finest statue I ever saw. I will not trouble you with a recapitulation of all that passed on her wedding night, and subsequently up to my arrival at Harpsdeen, because you, my sweet friend, doubtless know all that occurs on such occasions, but will confine myself to what I saw. She proposed to me to sleep in a room adjoining theirs, divided only by a thin oaken wainscot in which one of the knots in the wood could be taken out at pleasure and thus command a full view of the nuptial couch. Clara told me she would place a pair of wax lights on a table near the bed, and out of regard to me would so manage matters that I should see all that passed between her and her handsome husband, the squire. Accordingly, we all went to bed about ten o'clock one night and I, having undressed and wrapped myself in my *robe de chambre*, placed myself on an ottoman over against the panel. Assisted by her husband, Clara was soon reduced to a state of nature and stood naked like a beautiful Eve, with her lovely hair meandering down her alabaster back and shoulders.

' "Charles, dear," said my sweet friend, "do you lie on the foot of the bed and let me mount you, *à la* St George, you call it, I believe. I do so love that position."

'He kissed her tenderly, and being now himself naked, flung himself back on the foot of the bed.

'Then, dearest Maria, I saw, for the first time, that wondrous ivory staff with its ruby-crested head, rising from a nest of glossy black curls. Having waited a moment to give me an opportunity of seeing it, she pressed her face in his lap and took the head of his noble toy in her mouth; then after moistening it for a few seconds, she mounted astride him, displaying to my delighted gaze her large beautiful dimpled bottom and lily white thighs, between which I could clearly discern the mark of her sex; then grasping his wand in her little hand, she guided it in and immediately began to move up and down *à la postillon*.

'He clasped those white hemispheres with his hands, he squeezed them together, he held them open, he thrust his finger into the nether rosebud, he kissed her breasts, while mutual sighs of delight escaped the fond pair. As for me, I was so excited as to be almost beside myself, and felt almost suffocated. At length, I sought relief in the schoolgirl's substitute and used my finger for want of something better. Though this was but a poor expedient, it relieved the burning heat and caused a flow of love's dew, which allayed the itching desire which had taken possession of me Meantime, Clara's climax and Charlie's came simultaneously and they lay panting in each other's arms. In a very short time, however, he was again ready for action, and making Clara kneel upon the bed he stood behind, and again the amorous encounter was renewed. Four times in various attitudes did he repeat the play, and then putting out the candles they retired to rest.

'As for me, I could scarcely sleep at all; all night I was tossing about, trying in vain with my finger to procure myself that satisfaction which I had seen her enjoy.

'Now my dear Marie, inveigh as much as you please against love; for my part the sooner some nice young fellow takes a fancy to me the better I shall like it.'

'My dearest child,' cried the dark beauty, 'I dare say it is very true that your friend has made a very excellent match and is quite happy in her husband, but what I want to impress upon you is that for one such marriage as that there are ten wretched ones. Besides, I will, if you like, soon demonstrate to you that there is more pleasure to be derived from the love of woman for woman than any that the male can give. We are all alone here in this lovely glen; let me show you how I will make love.'

'You!' cried the young girl. 'What? Are you going then to make love to me?'

'To no other, my pet,' whispered hoarsely the salacious woman, as her dark eyes gleamed and her hand passed up the clothes of her companion.

'Oh; but,' said the younger, 'this is very droll, good heaven, what are you about! Really, Marie, I am surprised at you.'

'Do not be surprised any longer then, my little angel,' cried her friend. 'Give me your hand,' and she passed it up her own clothes. 'Now, I will show you how to touch that little secret part. It is not by putting the finger within that the pleasure is to be gained, but by rubbing it at the top, just at the entrance; there it is that nature has placed a nerve called by doctors the clitoris, and it is this nerve which is the chief seat of bliss in our sex.' All this while the libidinous creature was manipulating with skill.

The colour came and went in the cheeks of her beauteous companion, who faintly sighed out, 'Ah, Marie, what are you doing? Oh, joy; oh blissful sensation! Ah, is it possible – oh – oh – ur – r – r – r.' She could no longer articulate.

The tribade saw her chance, and waited no longer; throwing up the clothes of the young girl, she flew upon her like a panther, and forcing her face between the thighs of her friend, gamahuched her with inconceivable frenzy. Then, not satisfied with this, she pulled up her own clothes and straddled over the young girl, presenting her really symmetrically formed posteriors close to her face, nearly sitting down upon it in her eagerness to feel the touch of the young girl's tongue. Nor had she to wait long; wrought up to the last pitch of lascivious ecstasy, her friend would have done anything she required, and now gamahuched her to her heart's desire.

I continued to watch these tribades for some time, revolving in my mind how I could get possession of the young one, for whom I had conceived a most ardent longing.

Suddenly it occurred to me that, as they were strangers in the neighbourhood, it was not likely they had walked, and that possibly, on the outskirts of the wood, I should find a coach waiting for them.

Full of designs upon the pretty young creature, I left the amorous pair to their amusement and soon reached the margin of the road. Here, ere long, I espied a coach and six with servants in rich liveries, and approaching nearer saw from the coronet on the door that it belonged to some person of quality. As I came up I accosted one of the lackeys, and tossing him a crown, asked whose carriage it was.

'His Grace the Duke of G—'s, your honour,' said the man, touching his hat respectfully as he glanced at my embroidered coat, sword and diamond buckles and pocketed the crown.

'Then you are waiting, I presume, for the two ladies in the wood?' said I.

'Yes, sir,' replied the lackey; and being a talkative, indiscreet person, he added, 'Lady Cecilia Clairville, his grace's daughter, your honour, and Madame La Conte, her governess.'

'Ah, indeed!' said I, with as indifferent a manner as I could assume, and passed on.

At a turn of the road, I again dived into the wood and soon reached my own demesne.

'A very pretty affair, truly,' said I to myself as I took a glass of wine. Madame La Conte, engaged by the duke to complete the education of his daughter, takes advantage of her position to corrupt her, and by making her a tribade renders her wretched for life; for let me tell you, Sappho, there is no more certain road to ill health, loss of beauty, pleasure, and all the zest of life, than this horrid lust for the wrong sex.

'Very well, Madame La Conte,' I soliloquised, 'I shall turn this discovery to account, you may depend'; and with that resolve I went to bed.

Next morning I sent a billet in French by a trusty messenger to his grace's mansion in Cavendish Square. It ran as follows:

Madame, to all that passed between you and the lady Cecilia in the wood yesterday I was a witness. I am a man of position, and if you do not wish me to call upon the duke and acquaint him with your nefarious proceedings, you will come tomorrow afternoon at three o'clock to the big oak at the east end of the same wood, in a hackney coach, which you will alight from at the west side. To avoid discovery you had better both be masked.

Yours, as you behave yourself,

ARGUS

Punctual to the appointment I had made, I placed myself beneath the shade of the oak and, as there was no saying what might happen, or what ambush this devil of a Frenchwoman might lay for me, I armed myself with my sword and put in my pocket a brace of loaded pistols. Soon the fair creatures approached, hand in hand. I raised my hat to the young girl, but as for madame, I merely honoured her with a contemptuous stare.

'Do not be alarmed, Lady Cecilia,' said I; 'you are with a man of honour, who will do you no harm. As for you, madame, you may make a friend or an enemy of me, which you will.'

'Really, monsieur,' said the governess, 'your conduct in this affair is so singular that I know not what to think; but let me tell you, sir, that if you have any improper designs in inveigling us to this place, I shall know how to be avenged.'

'Doubtless, doubtless, madame; I know the French well and have well prepared for all contingencies. But allow me, ladies, to offer each an arm, and do me the honour to walk a little further into the wood.'

The alacrity with which the wily Frenchwoman complied told me at once what I had to expect.

She had resolved to assassinate me. Having made up my mind how I should act, I allowed her to lead me which way she pleased, keeping, however, a sharp look out on all sides as we strolled along. I was about to enter upon the subject of their coming, when suddenly three masked highwaymen sprang out, and demanding, 'Your money or your life,' levelled their horse pistols at us. The ladies screamed; I shook them both off, and as one of the scoundrels sent a bullet through my wig, I drew my pistols from my pocket and shot him dead; his companions then both fired and while one of the bullets grazed my shoulder, the other, curious enough, pierced the head of Madame La Conte, who, casting a glance full of fury upon me and clenching her hands, fell back a corpse.

The remaining rascals turned to flee but before they could escape I brought down the second with a bullet, and passed my sword through the lungs of the third.

The enemy being now utterly defeated, I turned towards the lovely Lady Cecilia, who had fainted, and raising her light form in my arms, bore her off to the spot where the coach had been left. But it was gone. The jarvey, doubtless hearing the firing and anxious to save his skin, had driven away. My resolution was taken in a moment. Carrying my fair burthen to the nearest gate that opened into my grounds, I bore her to my secret chamber and, having fetched old Jukes and Phoebe to her assistance, with strict orders not to tell her where she was but to pay her all needful attention, I saddled a swift horse and rode off to the nearest town, one of the magistrates there being an old friend .

He was much pleased to see me, but wondered at my being covered with dust and at my sudden arrival. I told him a most dreadful affair had happened: that returning home, I had heard cries for assistance in the wood, and had found three ruffians robbing and ill using some ladies; that they had fired at and wounded me and killed one of the ladies; that the other lady had escaped; that in the end I had succeeded in dispatching the rascals, more in consequence of their want of skill in the use of their weapons than from any extraordinary valour on my part; and finally I requested him to give orders to have the bodies removed with a view to a coroner's inquest. All of which he promised to do; and in spite of his earnest request that I should stay and drink a bottle of wine, I made my excuses and returned home.

I found my fair guest much better, and, having consoled her as well as I could for the loss of Madame La Conte, I then gradually unfolded to her all the wickedness of that vile woman and, after delicately touching upon the scene in the wood the day before, told her I had been a witness of it all and heard all the conversation.

At this denouement, Lady Cecilia covered her face with her hands to hide her blushes; and when I enquired whether Madame La Conte had shown her my letter, she said she knew madame had received a letter, which was very unpleasant and which she tore up and burnt in a great rage, but as to its contents she was ignorant.

This was very satisfactory news for me, as my handwriting might have been recognised. So turning to the young girl with a cheerful countenance, said, laughingly, 'Well, my dear young friend, all is well that ends well; now let us make plans for the future. In the first place, it seems to me that you are formed for the joys of love. It is true I am not quite so young a lover as you might desire; but I am more fit for amorous combats than many younger men. I am rich, and though not absolutely a man of rank I am a scion of a noble house. What do you say? I know your secret. I have already seen all your charms; shall we make a match of it? Will you marry me?'

'Indeed, sir,' said the dear girl, 'your gallantry in attacking those ruffians and defending my honour would alone have been sufficient to win my heart; but as my father, the duke, has designs of wedding me to a man older than himself, an old creature whom I detest, I deem this meeting with you a most fortunate one and will accept your offer with the same ingenuous frankness with which you have made it. You say, truly, that you have already viewed my person with pleasure; take it, dear sir, and do what you please with me. I am yours forever.'

I was quite enraptured with this decision, and it was determined that the duke should be written to in the morning and informed that his daughter, entertaining an insuperable objection to the match he had in store for her, had eloped with the man of her choice.

This affair settled, and Phoebe with many sly glances having made up a bed on one of the sofas, I shut the windows and hastened to undress my future bride. She was exquisitely formed, with the most lovely breasts in the world; and as for her bottom and thighs, nothing could be finer.

We were soon in bed, and all that her finger and the wanton tongue of madame had left of her maidenhead, I soon possessed myself of. Dawn found us still in dalliance; but at length, being both quite fatigued, with a last sweet kiss we fell asleep. The next day we were to be privately married by licence.

So now, my dear Sappho, I must conclude this long letter by saying to you, 'Do thou go and do likewise.'

❧§❧

To Julia

Your letter, giving me an account of your adventure with the Marquis at Ranelagh Gardens, diverted me vastly. Meantime, I have not been idle.

Since you were last here, I have colonised one corner of my grounds. A discreet old creature called Jukes has been placed in charge of that pretty cottage covered with roses and jasmine which you admired so much; and in the dairy she is assisted by the freshest and most charming of country girls. Positively you must come and pay me a visit, if only for the pleasure you will experience in the sight of Phoebe's perfections; but this is a digression and I know you hate digressions; therefore to proceed.

Phoebe and I, you must know, quite understand each other, but she is so pretty, brisk, loving and lively, and time, place and opportunity so frequently presented themselves, that I nearly killed myself with luscious fatigue and, having fucked her in every imaginable attitude, having gamahuched her and been gamahuched in return, I at length felt it begin to cloy and looked about for some new stimulant; but alas, Madame R did not call; I saw nothing of Mrs H. To write to them was not in accordance with my usual prudence. What was to be done? I was in despair. At this juncture, that dear old Jukes came to my aid, though very innocently, as I believe. With many curtseys and 'Hope your honour's worship won't be offended at my making so bold,' etc., she told me that she would be greatly beholden if I would allow her to have a little orphan grandchild of hers to live with her and Phoebe in the cottage.

She told me that her little girl was a sweet pretty creature, ten years of age, and as she knew that I liked to amuse myself with children sometimes (?), poor innocent soul, she thought I might like to have her.

I at once consented, and in a few days arrived one of the sweetest flowers that ever blushed unseen in the woods of Hampshire. I was charmed, and lost no time in providing suitable clothes for the little pet, and, with the aid of Phoebe, her frocks were so contrived that they only reached her knees. This, you will readily understand, was for the purpose of giving me facilities for seeing her young beauties without doing anything that might alarm her young innocence. We soon became great friends, and she took at once to Phoebe, the swing, the goldfish, strawberries and cream, the rambles in the woods and, above all, her handsome new clothes; all combined to render little Chloe as happy as a princess; while her old granddam would follow her about exclaiming, 'Lawk a mercy! well I never!' and so on.

In the course of a few days, our young rustic had quite rubbed off her first shyness and would run in and out of my room, sit on my knee, hide my snuff box, kiss me of her own accord and play all sorts of innocent tricks, like other children, in swinging, climbing up trees and tumbling about on the grass; the little puss not merely showing her legs but everything else besides.

At first Mrs Jukes tried to stop it, and told her it was rude to behave so before the gentleman, but I begged she would take no notice in future as I did not mind it and liked to see the little girl unrestrained and happy.

Now old Jukes always went to bed at sunset; I therefore arranged with Phoebe that after the old crone was gone to rest she should wash Chloe all over every night before putting her to bed; and that it might be done properly, I used to go and witness the operation, for it gave me a pleasurable sensation to see the child naked when Phoebe was present.

Phoebe was a clever girl and did not require much telling, so that none of the most secret charms of my little Venus were concealed from my lascivious gaze.

At one moment Phoebe would lay Chloe across her lap, giving me a full view of her little dimpled bum, holding open those white globes and exposing everything beneath. Then she would lay the girl on her back and spread out her thighs, as if to dry them with the towel. In fact, she put her into almost every wanton attitude into which she had seen me place myself. The little innocent girl, meanwhile, seemed to think this washing process capital fun, and would run and skip naked about the room in the exuberance of her animal spirits.

In this amusement I found all the excitement I desired, and should perhaps have been content with viewing her beauties without attacking her innocence but for a circumstance that occurred.

One evening, after the usual performance of washing, skipping about, etc., the little saucebox came and jumped on my knees, putting a leg on either side of them, and began courting a romp. Had I been a saint, whereas you know I am but a sinner, I could not have resisted such an attack on my virtue as this.

Only imagine, my dear Julia, this graceful lovely creature in all the bloom of early girlhood, stark naked except her stockings, her beautiful brown hair flowing over her exquisite shoulders; imagine her position, and how near she had placed herself to the fire and then, say, can you blame me?

In fine, I slid my hand down and released that poor stiff prisoner, who for the last half hour had nearly burst open his prison; as a natural consequence he slid along between her thighs and his crested head appeared (as I could see by the reflection in an old mirror) impudently showing his face, between her buttocks on the rear side. She would perhaps have noticed it, were it not that my finger had long been busy in her little slit already, 'tickling' as she called it, and she was laughing heartily and tickling me under the arms in return.

Suddenly, as if a thought struck her, she said, 'Do you know that – '
She paused. Never did man wait with more exemplary patience.
'That – that – '
Another pause.
'That I saw – '
Pause again.
'The cock – '
Here Phoebe tried to stop her, but she squeezed her interrupter's two cheeks so that she could not speak and hurriedly concluded, 'Making chickens – there.'

This was too much for my gravity, and I was convulsed with laughter; when I had a little recovered, I asked, 'And how does the cock do that, my dear?'

'Why,' said Chloe, with the most artless manner in the world, 'he tickles the hen, and when she lays eggs they come to chickens.'
'Tickles her! I do not understand,' said I.
'But he does,' insisted the little girl.
'But the cock has no fingers; how can he tickle?'
'Why,' cried Chloe triumphantly, 'he has got a finger, and a long one too, and I saw it shoot from under his tail when he was treading the hen, and he tickled her, just as you are tickling me now, but putting it right into her body. Now, am I not right in saying the cock makes chickens by tickling the hen?'

'Well reasoned, my little logician,' cried I, really pleased with her wit. 'I see, though you have lived in the country, you are no fool, and I will tell you something which little girls are always very curious about but which their mothers and grannies will never tell them anything of. But first tell me why you thought the cock tickling the hen made the chickens.'

'Why, because Phoebe told me, to be sure.'

'Oh, ho!' said I, laughing. 'You told her, Phoebe, did you?'

Poor Phoebe looked frightened out of her wits.

'I hope you will forgive me, sir, but Chloe did worrit so and keep all on about that ere beast of a cock, that at last I up and told her.'

'God bless you, my dear girl. What if you did? There is no harm in that, I hope. There can never be anything wrong in what is natural.'

Then turning to Chloe, whose little cunny I had not let go of all this while, 'Would you like to know, my dear, where the babies come from and how they are made?'

'Oh, yes; that I just should,' exclaimed Chloe, hugging and kissing me.

'Very well; now you know, I suppose, that you are not made exactly like a little boy, do you not?'

'Yes, I know that. Down here, you mean,' and she pointed to where my finger was still tickling.

'Just so. But did you ever, by chance, happen to see a man?'

'Never.'

'And you would like to?'

'Of all things.'

'There then!' cried I, lifting her up and allowing the rampant yard to spring up against my belly.

'Oh, the funny thing!' said Chloe; then taking hold of it, 'How hot it is. That is what I have felt against my bottom these last ten minutes and could not think what it was; but what has that to do with making babies?'

'I will show you,' said I, 'but I cannot promise you that I shall make one, as I am too old for that, but it is by doing what I am going to do to Phoebe that children are begotten.'

'Oh, I see!' cried the little girl, clapping her hands, 'you are going to serve Phoebe as I saw the stallion serve the mare today. That will be capital fun.'

'Serve the mare,' I ejaculated, glancing over my shoulder at Phoebe. 'How's this?'

'Well, the truth is, sir,' said the self-conscious girl, 'ever since your honour showed me that trick I have often gone to see them do it, and I was watching them today when this little scapegrace came running into the stable. So I was obliged to tell her all about it, as I did about the chickens.'

'Well,' said I, 'if she has seen that, I see no harm in her seeing the other; so pull up your clothes, my dearest creature.'

In a moment Phoebe had tucked up her petticoats and, kneeling on the truckle bed and jutting her white posteriors well out, presented a full view of all her charms. 'Oh, my,' cried Chloe, 'why Phoebe, you have got hair growing on your – '

She stopped, and with a charming blush, hid her face in my bosom.

'And so will you have, my little maid,' I whispered, 'when you are as old as she is; but now observe what I am going to do, and mind you tickle me underneath all the while.'

This she did in the most delightful manner, occasionally laughing to see Phoebe wriggling about. As soon as all was over, I sent Phoebe to my room for some refreshments and wine, and while she was gone I gamahuched the lovely little Chloe, which operation, coming as it did after all the frigging she had undergone, roused at once her dormant passions into precocious energy. With eagerness she seized my again erect wand, and putting it into her little mouth, worked it up and down so that, just as Phoebe returned, I sent a spirting shower over her tongue while her virgin dew drenched my own.

'Oh, my! how salty it is,' sputtered the little girl, spitting and making a wry face. 'And is it that stuff, sir, that makes the babies?'

'One drop of it, my dear, is sufficient to make a little girl as pretty as you.'

'Or a little boy?'

'Yes, or a little boy.'

After supper, Chloe, who said she was not at all sleepy, wanted Phoebe and me to perform again, but I told her that was quite enough for one night and that she was on no account to say anything of what she had seen to her granddam.

Now I think, my dear Julia, you will say I have related a most interesting adventure; but really, I wish you would come and stay a few days and share in our sports. I shall confidently expect to see you before long.

◈⚬◈

To Euphrosyne

Your pretty cousin Sappho will doubtless have told you the startling news, that I am – what do you think? – married! It is true, however, and a very charming little creature my wife is, I can tell you.

Quite free from all those silly notions of propriety and jealousy, her chief delight is to make me happy, not only by giving up to me her own pretty person but by throwing in my way any chance that may occur when there is any new face that pleases me.

With this view, she proposed to me that we should adopt the two little daughters of a cousin of hers. Being poor, he had accepted a situation in the East India Company's service, and subsequently contracted, in the East, an imprudent marriage of which these children were the fruits. Their mother being dead, he sent them home to be educated; and by a singular chance they were placed at the school of Mrs J, who you know is a tenant of mine and occupies that house near this place which I offered to your papa some years ago.

Of course, after my marriage I presented Cecilia to my household as their mistress, no object being gained by keeping it a secret, and there is a great convenience in this since, whatever they may have thought before about the secret chamber and grounds, as my wife is now with me it silences scandal at once. Now I will go on to relate to you the acquisition this plan of my wife's has produced.

We drove over to Mrs J, with whom I was always a favourite; and with reason, as more than once when she was a little straitened for her rent I have sent her a receipt for the money without ever receiving it.

She is the widow of a naval officer, and though over five and thirty years of age, has the remains of considerable personal attractions.

She was at home and delighted with our visit. So we opened the object of it.

'My dear Mrs J,' began Lady Cecilia with the smile of a seraph, 'I have persuaded Sir Charles to allow me to adopt my poor cousin's little girls, and I now intend to take the entire charge of these young ladies.'

Then, observing Mrs J begin to look very thoughtful, she quickly added, 'But do not misunderstand me. I mean not to remove them from your excellent supervision; their education must of course proceed as usual. All I want is permission to break through one of your rules and ask you to let them come and pass a few days with us sometimes, instead of coming for the regular holidays.'

'I am sure,' cried Mrs J, whose countenance had quite cleared up during this speech, 'I shall be vastly pleased to oblige your ladyship in any way in my power. Pray arrange it just as you like.'

'And if,' added I, 'my dear Mrs J, you will yourself occasionally favour us with your company and bring any of your young ladies with you, we shall both, I am sure, be enchanted. You know I have some pretty grounds to which I do not admit everybody, but your name will be an "open sesame" at all times.'

'Oh, Sir Charles,' cried the good lady with a conscious blush (which showed she knew those precincts well), 'you are too good, I am sure. But really, to tell you the truth, I was quite frightened when I saw your carriage drive up the avenue, as I remembered I am two quarters' rent in arrears; indeed, I am afraid you find me a sorry tenant.'

'I would not change you, my dear madam, for all the best tenants in the world. But see, I anticipated your fears, well knowing the sensibility of your nature and your honourable sentiments; here is the receipt, and as for the money, pray accept it to procure any little article of jewellery you may require.'

Mrs J glanced furtively at my wife before she replied; but seeing nothing in that sweet face but the most amiable and charming smile she said at once, 'Oh, Sir Charles! how very considerate and kind you are; always the same noble gentleman, madam,' she continued, turning to Lady Cecilia, 'so kind, so generous.'

'Then it is all settled,' said Cecilia; 'and remember to bring some of the prettiest of your young ladies. You know Sir Charles loves a good romp with young girls, and I am not at all jealous.'

'Oh, my lady, I can see you are a sweet creature, and I am delighted Sir Charles has made such a happy choice. I will bring two or three of my girls with your dear little cousins; but will you not see them before you go?'

'Oh, yes, certainly; send for them, I beg.'

Mrs J rang the bell, and presently appeared two of the most lovely, blooming children I had ever seen. Augusta and Agnes they were called, one nine and the other eleven years old. They had the sweetest and most innocent countenances in the world, and their manners did ample justice to Mrs J's training. I took one on each knee, and as I kissed their rosy cheeks I felt through both their muslin frocks that they both had nice, firm, plump little bottoms, with which I hoped ere long to be better acquainted.

Mrs J saw the movement, and smiled archly. Then, catching Cecilia's eye, 'A sad man! a sad rake! is he not, my lady?'

'Oh, indeed he is!' cried Cecilia, laughing; 'and if I mistake not, you and I know all about it, *n'est-ce pas?*'

Mrs J blushed scarlet, but seeing that the remark was mere playful badinage and not malicious, she soon recovered her presence of mind. After a merry chat with the little girls, a tip for them of a guinea a piece, and the promise of new dolls, we took our leave.

As soon as we were in the carriage my wife gave me a tap with her fan, saying, 'Positively, Charles, you are incorrigible; I do verily believe that Mrs J is an old flame of yours.'

'Of course she is, my love; and a deuced fine woman she was, I can assure you; a little stale now, perhaps, but a most useful person, and so prudent. Whenever she has had any orphan girls, or girls whose friends did not pay well or punctually, if they were pretty (and she will not take ugly ones), she has always brought them to me; and in this way for five guineas I have bought many a little maidenhead of her. Yet so cleverly has she managed matters that nothing unpleasant has ever arisen out of these affairs. Except, indeed, in one case which I had almost forgotten, which was rather awkward, as the fool off a guardian thought proper to take offence upon his ward complaining to him; and he came down here in a towering passion with Frank Firebrace of the Guards. He waited in the wood and sent the captain to me with a cartel.

'I was not the man to refuse such a summons, but told him he must wait till I also sent for a friend. I knew where an old chum of mine was to be found and posted off a messenger for him. On his arrival we started to the place of rendezvous, and there, on that deep dell which you admire so much, I was under the disagreeable necessity of killing the guardian of the little girl while O'Brien made an end of poor Firebrace. I was vexed with him, I remember, for this, but he quieted me with, "Don't you see, my dear fellow, in a delicate affair like this, there is nothing like securing silence; and sure dead men tell no tales, at all, at all." As for the girl, we smuggled her out of the country and locked her up in a convent. Egad, it was a deuced unpleasant business and made poor Mrs J very much afraid of Bridewell, at the time.'

'Oh! dear Charles,' said Cecilia, 'how charmingly wicked you are, and how vastly cool you seem to speak of it. You naughty man, I do believe you ravished the girl.'

'Oh, yes,' said I, 'it was doubtless what the law called a rape.'

'And what had Mrs J to do with it?'

'Ah, she brought the girl to me and held her down while I deflowered her. You see the girl was a little Puritan whom we had, in vain, tried to break in; but her modesty was superior to either menaces or presents. Unfortunately, she was very beautiful, and only thirteen, and the opposition made me mad for her. But do not let us speak of it any more; it was one of those contretemps which occasionally mar the uniform career of a man of pleasure.'

'Really, Charles, you quite frighten me with your coolness. But never mind, you dear man, I love you with all my heart and shall never think very harshly of your little peccadilloes.'

The following Thursday brought Mrs J, the two young cousins, and three other young ladies about whom it will be necessary to say a few words.

Miss Marshall was a poor Irish girl from the county of Kerry, whose unnatural father, a naval officer, having placed her three years before with Mrs J, had never paid a shilling. Upon writing to the town where she came from, Mrs J found that her father was her only relative in the world. and looked upon her, therefore, as lawful prey.

This girl was a thorough Irish beauty, with dark blue eyes and black hair, a rather dingy skin, a pretty enough face, and a well-formed figure, though rather thin; there was something taking about her, although she looked grave and sad. She was turned twelve years old.

The next I shall describe was Miss Jennings, a merry, laughing blonde, very plump and pretty, with a profusion of light hair. She had been brought up by her grandmother, who paid very little. This girl was about eleven and ripe for a frolic.

The last of the trio, Miss Bellew, was a tall, handsome girl of fifteen, nicely made, but a little too slight if anything. She was dark and swarthy, a brunette, in fact; but there was soul in her black eyes, and withal a look of languor quite enchanting. As for the little cousins, they were chubby children.

Such being our party, and chocolate and fruit with plenty of cakes and bonbons being served on the lawn by Phoebe and Chloe, we all soon became friends. The refection concluded, and leaving Cecilia to entertain Mrs J, I took the bevy of young girls to see the poultry yard and then the ponies. I had previously given Phoebe a hint to let the stallion into the mare's compartment, so that when we arrived the animals were in the very act – a sight which provoked the astonishment and laughter of the little girls and made Miss Marshall look very pale and grave while the Misses Jennings and Bellew blushed up to the eyes.

'Oh, come away, come away,' cried Miss Marshall, turning sharp round; but I stopped her.

'Why should they go away, my dear?' I asked.

'Because, because – ' and then stopped.

'Because what?' said I.

'Because – I think you are a naughty bad man, Sir Charles,' sobbed the foolish girl, and burst into tears.

'Oh Bella,' cried all the other girls in a breath, 'for shame, to speak so to Sir Charles. Never mind her, sir, she is always like that, a miserable thing to spoil fun.'

'I am sorry to hear it,' said I. 'When I invite young ladies here I expect them to be cheerful and polite, and if they are not we have a birch rod quite handy.'

Mrs J coming up at this moment, the girls all ran to tell her how Bella had behaved.

'In that case, Sir Charles,' said the good lady, 'we must commence the sports by giving her a good flogging.'

Miss Marshall turned paler than she was before at this announcement. Mrs J had a heavy hand, as she knew by dear-bought experience, but she was of a dogged and sulky disposition and said nothing.

'How now, miss,' cried Mrs J, 'say you are very sorry immediately or you shall be flogged at once.'

No answer.

'Will you apologise or not?'

No answer.

'Yes, yes; I see we must make you speak then. Here, my good girl,' said she, addressing Phoebe. 'You are strong, take her up; and you, my little lasses, come, hold her legs.'

And the refractory Bella being mounted, and her clothes thrown over her head, Mrs J selected from a new birch broom a goodly handful of twigs and, tying them with a ribband, prepared for action.

We all now had a full view of her well-formed white buttocks and thighs; and the other girls, who seemed to enjoy the scene, held her legs so wide apart that we could see her pouting cunny and all the regions thereabout.

Bella, meanwhile, bounding and struggling to be free, only exposed her charms the more.

'Now,' said Mrs J, 'you young hussy, for whom I have never yet received a shilling, I'll teach you manners, you wretched pauper, I will.'

And she commenced flogging her till the stubborn girl roared for mercy and her white bottom glowed again.

'No – no – no,' cried Mrs J, giving a tremendous cut each time she said the word, 'I will flog this devil out of you before I have done.'

'Oh, dear madam, pray forgive me. Oh – oh – oh – oh; kind Sir Charles, do intercede! Oh, I shall die; oh! oh!'

But by this time I had got too much interested to interfere and quieted Cecilia with a gesture, and the operation proceeded.

Large weals rose up on her flesh, the blood started and ran down her thighs, and at length, with a prolonged shriek, she fainted.

'There,' cried Mrs J, drawing a long breath, 'take her away, and don't let me see the slut till it is time to leave.'

But at the sight of the poor fainting girl I relented, and lifting her up bore her to a couch in my room; and having unfastened her dress and bathed her temples with Hungary water, I left her and returned to my company. Preparations were just being made for a game at hunt-the-slipper, and everyone being seated on the lawn I ran round the circle, every now and then feeling for the slipper under the legs of the girls.

The little screams, the shouts of laughter, and the fun was tremendous; for you may be sure that every girl in her turn felt my hand between her naked thighs.

With some it was a hasty grasp, but with others I lingered and fairly frigged, pretending all the while that I was sure they had the slipper. To see the little Agnes and Augusta laugh at being so tickled was delightful; and the conscious blushes of the Misses Jennings and Bellew were equally enchanting. As for Miss Bellew, her languishing black eyes shot forth scintillations of light as she fairly spent in my hand; but the little Jennings was less precocious and merely laughed at the fun.

Altogether it was a most fucktious romp, and made me so amorous that I at length proposed a game of hide-and-seek for a change, and unperceived beckoned to Cecilia; we both ran to hide.

Having retired into a deep cluster of trees and shrubs, I put my little wife on her knees and was into her in a moment, at the same time calling out 'whoop'. Into the wood they all came shouting and laughing, but could not for a long time find us; at length Agnes and Augusta taking an opposite vista to their companions, came suddenly upon us just as my climax came. I immediately drew out, and thus gave them a complete view of that red headed staff, at the sight of which, and of their cousin's ivory posteriors shining in the sun, they stopped, turned round, and bounded off to their companions, crying out:

'Oh! Miss Jennings, oh Miss Bellew, here's Sir Charles doing to cousin Cecilia just what the horse did to the mare!'

Then we heard a whispering; and presently I became aware, by the rustling of the branches, that the girls were placing themselves in ambush to see all they could.

The idea of such beauteous spectators brought me up to the mark again in a moment, and at it we went in good style. Every now and then a little eager face would peep out from among the leaves and then be withdrawn in great trepidation, which caused such a thrill to run through my veins that I brought that second embrace to a conclusion much sooner than I had a mind to.

No sooner did they see that I was beginning to button up again but they scampered off in different directions, pretending to be looking for us. Meanwhile, we shifted our quarters and again cried out 'whoop'.

This time they ran up to catch us, pretending, the little sly pussies, that they had had such a hunt for us. It being now Miss Bellew's turn to hide, we all remained on the lawn while she ran into the wood. It now occurred to me for the first time that Mrs J and Phoebe had disappeared, nor could I anywhere see Chloe.

So when Miss Bellew's 'whoop' summoned us to the wood, instead of looking for her I hunted in every direction for the truants and, at length, at some distance from the spot where the game was going on, I fancied I saw a bit of blue silk between the trees; bending my steps to a thick clump of hazel, I approached softly, and lo! on a little patch of mossy turf, in a hollow space, I espied the excellent Mrs J doing a little bit of tribadism with Phoebe. They were at the height of enjoyment, Phoebe uppermost.

'Ah, ah, my sweet girl,' Mrs J was sighing out. 'That is it. Ah, ah, now you've found the right place, at the – top. Oh, bliss; ah-oh. Ur-r-r! Oh, how nice; continue to roll your tongue round and round.'

Then slapping the beautiful great white bottom of Phoebe, which was presented to her, she continued, 'Oh, what heavenly charms, what a skin! what glorious white globes! what a delicious little nether mouth, let me kiss your sweet cunny; let me thrust my tongue in and taste your spendings. Ah, this is bliss indeed. Ur-r-r-r!'

Then Phoebe began.

'Ah, dear madam, what are you doing? oh lud, it do make me feel so funny loike. Oh, my, ain't it nice though? Oh – '

A gush of spending from Mrs J stopped her mouth, while the movements became furious. Phoebe rolled off on to the grass and the two women lay without sense or motion beyond the heaving of their breasts. I was much amused and retreated without being discovered.

I now thought of Chloe, and wanting my snuffbox which I had left indoors, I went to get it; the first thing that met my eyes was the little girl trying to console the naughty Miss Marshall, who was lying on her side on a couch, with her face to the wall, while the good-natured Chloe was bathing the poor flayed bum of the young lady.

I approached softly, and with my finger on my lip motioned to Chloe to take no notice, and seated myself about a yard from them.

As Miss Marshall's clothes were turned up above her waist, I was able to contemplate at my ease the symmetrical proportions of her sylph-like form.

The fine contour of her virgin rose and the little rosebud attached thereto, all was before me.

Presently she spoke. 'How kind you are to me, dearest Chloe,' she said, languidly. 'I begin to feel in less pain now, but what is very singular is that I, who never had any sensations in that part before, now feel a most singular itching between the legs – in the slit, you know.'

'Just here?' cried Chloe, laughing and putting her finger in.

'Oh, yes, yes. Ah, how nice it feels now you touch it. Oh, I feel so ashamed,' and she covered her face with her hand.

Chloe withdrew her hand.

'I did not mean to offend you,' she said.

'Offend me; oh, no. Let me feel that dear little finger again.'

I approached on my hands and knees and quickly substituted my finger for Chloe's.

'Oh, my dear girl,' she cried, 'oh, how very nice, but I feel quite ashamed.'

Then, as I touched her clitoris, a shiver ran through her frame. She threw herself over on her back, expanded her thighs, and, with her eyes still closed, murmured, 'Come, come here, darling girl, on my bosom, on my bosom.'

I placed Chloe there in a moment, and then tossing up the little girl's clothes, I began toying with her lovely buttocks. Then, kneeling up behind her, I directed my fiery steed strait at Miss Marshall's maiden-head.

The first push took me in about an inch, but, with a shriek and a start, the Irish girl opened her eyes, commencing with, 'Oh, my dear Chloe, how you hurt me, I – '

Then seeing me she turned pale with terror and struggled to get up.

'Oh, for heaven's sake, let me get up – oh, goodness! Mercy! mercy!'

These ejaculations followed every thrust, for I would not let go but made Chloe lie with all her weight on the little Marshall until I was at length fairly into her body. Then, indeed, I rolled Chloe on one side and extending myself on the bosom of the girl and grasping her tightly in my arms I consummated the defloration.

At first terrified, then angry, she finished by hugging her ravisher in her arms and covering him with kisses.

All this, which has taken so long to tell, happened in an incredibly short space of time, so that I was hardly missed ere I reappeared among my young friends.

Mrs J and Phoebe now joined us, looking very innocent, and I having interceded for Miss Marshall, she and Chloe were sent for and joined in the sports. I had quite tamed the angry petulant girl and she occasionally glanced at me with a look full of meaning and of indefinable tenderness. Her passions were aroused and she had tasted of the tree of knowledge.

It being now eight o'clock, supper was served up to us with a profusion of all the delicacies of the season and the choicest wines and liqueurs. After this we had a dance and a game at blind-man's-buff, and then my guests took their departure, Mrs J declaring that she had never enjoyed herself more! (Glancing at Phoebe.)

'Well then,' said I, 'suppose you all come again next Thursday?'

'Oh, I shall be enchanted, I am sure, to do so, Sir Charles,' said Mrs J, 'but I suppose you will not want to see Miss Marshall any more?'

'On the contrary,' I remarked, 'she has quite made the *amende honorable*, and we are now very good friends. Is it not so, young lady?' I added, turning to her.

A burning blush suffused her pale face, but she managed to stammer out, 'Oh, yes, Madame, I am sure Sir Charles is most kind. I am very sorry I behaved as I did, but if you will let me come next time I promise never so to offend again, even if there are fifty horses and mares instead of one.'

With that I kissed them all round, and handing them into my coach bid them good-night.

Adieu, dear friend.

To Lais

Lady Cecilia has fallen in love, and with a very Daphnis too, the beautiful little brother of the charming Phoebe. He came here the other day to see his sister, and prodigiously took the fancy of my lady. As we are far too philosophical, in this our terrestrial paradise, to agitate ourselves with such absurd passions as jealousy, I left Cecilia to do as she liked; so she has engaged the pretty fellow, who is just fourteen and the image of his sister, as her body page, but instead of putting him in livery, has dressed him *à la* Watteau, a style of costume at once simple and elegant.

Of course, she made his sister give him a good scrubbing and combing before he mounted his new clothes, and now powdered, perfumed and dressed he looks fit for a princess. Phoebe is hugely pleased that Jack is to stay here, and as for little Chloe, she evidently has some very sinister designs on his virtue.

I told Cecilia that I congratulated her on such an acquisition and hoped she would not object to my seeing some of the performances. She laughed, and replied, 'Oh, see all you like, my dear Charles, only don't let the boy know at first, as he is very bashful and timid.'

I promised compliance.

A few days afterwards, as I lay on the banks of the lake listlessly feeding the carp, Phoebe came running to me, and having seated herself quite out of breath by my side, she told me that Cecilia and her brother were amusing themselves in the grotto, in the grove of beeches, and if I would make haste I might see something that would amuse me. So, throwing my arm round Phoebe's waist, I accompanied her, going round to the opposite side to the entrance. We looked through a chink in the rockwork and could both see and hear all that passed.

First I observed Cecilia seated on the mossy bank, and holding the boy, whose breeches were down, between her naked thighs. His hands were toying with her bubbies while she, having tucked up his fine cambric shirt, with her right hand caressed his little stiff thing and with her left patted his pretty dimpled soft and girlish bottom.

'Oh, you dear little fellow,' said she, 'what a beautiful figure you have got, your waist is so small, your bottom so plump, dimpled, and rounded, and your skin so soft; you have such a lovely face, your hair is so silky, luxuriant and beautiful, and you have such little hands and feet, surely nature quite intended you for a girl, only she gave you this little saucy cock instead of something else, which, however, I am very glad of, as you will be able to play with me. Dear boy, do you like me to tickle it?'

'Oh, yes, my lady,' cried the lad, 'very much indeed, and I do love these little breasts so, do let me kiss them.'

And pulling her bubbies out he buried his face between them.

'But,' she exclaimed, 'you have not looked at this other little secret place – but perhaps, you have seen girls before?'

'Why, my lady, to say the truth, I have, but only little ones. I should like to see your ladyship's beautiful cunt very much.'

'Oh, fie, naughty boy, do not use such naughty words. But look, here it is.'

And she straddled open her legs.

'Feel it with your pretty little hand. Oh, you dear fellow, that is nice; now lie down upon me and I will show you what love is.'

And grasping his beautiful buttocks, she drew him to her and he slipped in with ease.

'Now, dear boy, move up and down, that's it, my little stallion; you are, I see, an apt pupil.'

Then holding open those white hemispheres, she inserted her delicate finger into his little rosy orifice behind, and entwining her lovely limbs round his loins, they were presently bounding and heaving with delight.

The sight was so exhilarating to both Phoebe and myself that I lifted up her clothes, and still contemplating the ardent young lovers, commenced the same game myself.

Now, whatever the ancients may have thought on the subject, I must confess I have never seen what the peculiar point of attraction could be in having beautiful boys, as they unquestionably did; yet when I saw that lovely young bottom bounding up and down, and Cecilia's wanton finger frigging away, a strange dizziness seized me and I felt a lust, stronger than the lust for women, lay hold of me.

But one cannot be perfectly happy in this world long together, so that it happened that just at the height of titillation, my climax came and I sent a gushing stream into her bowels.

Cecilia and her Daphnis having also died away in bliss, we beat a retreat, to prevent discovery.

Thus you see, my dear Lais, that like a true Epicurean, I never let slip any pleasure within my reach.

I think it behoves us to live while we may and give full scope to those delicious sensual appetites which we can only enjoy for so short a time.

Hoping soon to have the happiness of seeing you here,

I remain,

Your devoted Admirer.

To Thalia

I believe, my dear girl, I gave you a full relation of all that had passed here during this last three months on the occasion of that delicious clandestine visit you paid me about a week ago. I am now going to continue the narrative, which I hope will prove edifying to my dear little girl .

You must know then, my love, that I was most anxious to become better acquainted with my wife's young cousins, and as she was quite willing I should do just as I liked with them, I sent a letter to Mrs J requesting that they might pass a few days with us. They arrived accordingly the next morning.

'Now, Cecilia,' said I, 'I want you to leave us entirely to ourselves; so do you go and make a few calls in the neighbourhood.'

To this the dear little wife at once consented, so taking each of my little cousins by the hand, I proposed we should go a nutting (you know what a famous nut wood I have here). The little creatures were delighted and skipped merrily along. Arrived at the wood, they began climbing the trees in search of the nuts, showing me their little fat bottoms and legs without the least concern.

As soon as they had gathered a pretty considerable basketful, I proposed that we should seat ourselves under a spreading tree and eat them.

'Now, my little loves,' said I, 'while you are cracking your nuts, I will try and amuse you.'

The pretty creatures in seating themselves drew up their legs so as to make a lap to hold their nuts, and as Mrs J had taken care their petticoats should be short, I had a full view of all their youthful charms. Plump, white little thighs, between which pouted their rosy slits, a luscious sight, enough to fire the veins of an anchorite.

But, as I have no pretensions to that holy character, I was beside myself with desire and ready to eat them up altogether. However, I restrained my impatience with much ado and began to beat about the bush.

'Now I daresay, my darlings, you would like to know where the babies come from?'

'Oh!' cried the little Agnes, 'I know very well.' Then whispering mysteriously in my ear, 'They come out of the parsley bed.'

'Nonsense,' cried Augusta, who had overheard her, 'no such thing, I know better than that; they come from the mother, do they not, Sir Charles?'

'Yes, my dear,' said I sententiously, 'indeed they do; but can you tell me how they got into the mother's stomach in the first place, and how they get out in the second?'

'Why, no, Sir Charles, I cannot tell what made them get there, nor do I exactly know how they come into the world; some of the girls at our school say that the mother's stomach opens and lets them out, but I really do not quite know.'

'Would you like me to tell you, then?'

'Oh, dear sir, of all things, do, do, tell us all about it.'

'Well, then,' said I, laughing, 'I must begin at the beginning.'

'Yes, yes, that's it,' cried the little girls in a breath, cracking their nuts and very wickedly throwing the shells at an unoffending sparrow who was hopping about near them.

'Very well,' said I. 'In the beginning the heaven and the earth were created – '

'Oh, lud, we know all about that, you see. But what has that got to do with it?' cried the saucy Augusta.

'In the beginning the heaven and the earth were created,' I went on, dogmatically, 'every creeping thing and all that therein is, male and female. Now, can you tell me why they were made male and female?'

My young pupils looked puzzled.

'I will tell you,' said I gravely, 'they were made male and female that they may be joined together, just as you saw the pony stallion and the mare joined, and thus propagate their kind. There is nothing wrong or indelicate in their doing this; are we not told to "be fruitful and multiply"?'

'Of course we are,' cried the girls in a breath.

'Well, then,' I continued, 'Miss Marshall was wrong in wishing you to come away the other day, for, my dear children, you were contemplating one of the works of nature. Now you know, I dare say, that little boys are not made like little girls?'

'Oh, yes; we know that.'

'Well, shall I tell you why they are not?'

'Oh, yes; do, do.'

'Well then, because that little innocent thing of the boy's is capable, in the man, of becoming a great thing, and nature has ordained that he shall feel a particular pleasure in putting that part of him into that little female opening, of which I see two specimens before me.'

They both blushed and pulled down their clothes.

'When it is in, he moves up and down, and in doing so gives great pleasure to the female, and after a time he discharges into her a thick, milky, rather gruel-like fluid, which is the seed; this being received into the womb and fecundating the ovaries or eggs, which are in her fallopian tubes – so called from a learned doctor named Fallopius, who studied them – an egg descends into the womb and begins to grow, and nine months after a child is born.'

'Oh, but that is very funny, and very wonderful,' they cried .

'My dear girls, it is not funny, but it is wonderful.'

They both looked very thoughtful; at length Augusta said, 'And would there be any harm in your showing us what this wonderful thing which makes the babies is like?'

'On the contrary, my dear little girl, here it is!' and upon my unbuttoning my breeches, out sprang my truncheon as stiff as a carrot.

'Oh, gracious, what a funny thing,' was the ejaculation which escaped them as they approached and began to handle Mr Pasquin.

'That is the true maker of babies, my darlings, is he not a fine dolly? Play with him a little and soon you will see what the seed is like, and remember every drop may contain a baby.'

'Oh, the funny, big, red-headed thing,' exclaimed the little girls, rubbing and pulling it about. 'And what are these two balls for, Sir Charles?'

'They, my dears, contain the seed, which is formed in the loins at first, and then descending through those balls pass into the woman.'

'Then,' said Augusta, 'when people are said to be in love, it means that they want to join those parts together.'

'Just so, that is the end of all marriages.'

'But,' argued little Agnes, 'do ladies really like to have it done to them?'

'Of course they do, my dear, if they love the man they marry.'

'But why do they like it?'

'Because they feel a strange pleasure in the act.'

'Really, how very odd,' both exclaimed.

'Not at all,' said I, 'let me just tickle you a little in that part and you will soon know what I mean.'

'Indeed,' said Augusta, 'I know already, for when you did that to me while playing hunt-the-slipper, I thought it very nice.'

At this admission, as they had not ceased caressing that great erect prick, a *jet d'eau* spouted forth, covering both their hands with the warm fluid, at which they both gave a little scream of astonishment and then fell to examining it attentively.

'And every drop of this curious stuff contains a baby?' enquired Augusta.

'Every drop,' said I.

'Who would have thought it,' she continued, much interested, 'how very, very curious.'

'Having now told you all about that part of the business, my dear children,' said I, 'I must now go on to tell you that the pleasures of love are manifold, and I will explain to you what some of those pleasures are.

'First of all is the pleasure derived from titillation with the finger, as practised by schoolgirls. But this, though very exquisite when first commenced, palls after a year or two, deadens the sensation of the little cunny and, what is worse, injures the health. The blooming cheeks will then become pale, the bright eyes sunken, the skin yellow and flabby. Therefore that is not the enjoyment I intend to recommend to you, my dears.

'Secondly, there is tribadism, or the love of one girl for another, which leads them mutually to gratify each other's desires by kissing and licking that salacious part of their bodies. No doubt the bliss is great, but I never yet met a girl who would assert that a tribade could satisfy her. It is very exciting, no doubt, but after working the nervous sensibility up to the highest tension, it leaves you still tingling with desire – longing, wishing for something you know not what, but forever unsatisfied. Like that unhappy Tantalus, forever plunged to the chin in water but unable to drink; so I cannot recommend tribadism.

'Thirdly, there is the true and right kind of bliss, when two young creatures of opposite sexes meet, kiss, caress, coo and – time, place and opportunity occurring – join together those luscious parts of their persons. Add to this the pursuit of pleasure *en règle*, and to these delights of love I will introduce you.'

The little girls, who had paid great attention, came nestling up to me, saying, 'Oh, what a dear, nice man you are, Sir Charles; I do love you so very much, you are so kind.'

I kissed them both and, with my two hands patting each of their little peach-like nether beauties while they played with dolly of the red head, I continued, 'But before I introduce you to your young lover that is to be, I want to say a few words on incentives. Now, while I disapprove of fingering, tribadism, gamahuching and the like when intended as a sole means of satisfying natural lust, I think such acts may be practised if the natural completion in a hearty fuck is to follow.

'None of these acts will then do you the least harm, because the effect of fucking is to tranquillize the nerves and produce a delicious calmness and serenity. Having now, therefore, concluded my sermon, I will go without delay and find Master Jack, who I am very sure is up to some mischief, either stealing my peaches or fighting amain the cocks in the poultry yard, setting the dogs at old Mother Jukes' cat or teasing Chloe. However, I will bring him captive to your feet.'

I found our young Daphnis at the cottage. But let me describe him to you, for you did not see him when here.

You are to imagine then, a beautiful young girl, but with male, instead of female, attributes, with a polished skin like alabaster, and whose exquisite face is a perfect oval; imagine a girl of fourteen with large melting eyes, black lashes, pencilled eyebrows, *nez retroussé*, small coral-lipped mouth, teeth like pearls, and dimpled cheeks tinted with the softest blush of the rose.

Imagine a profusion of light brown curling hair, powdered and tied by a cherry-coloured ribbon, rather narrow chest, small waist, and voluptuous hips and accessories; in fine a charming picture, full of grace and elegance, dressed *à la* Watteau.

I found the young rascal lying at the foot of a cherry tree, up which Chloe had clambered, lazily eating the fruit she threw down to him, while ever and anon he languidly raised his eyes to look at that other fruit which her short dress rendered so conspicuous.

As I conducted him into the nut wood, the two sweet children ran to meet us, and then looked shy, shook their shoulders and blushed. Not so the boy; he went up to them with some gallant speech or other not now worth repeating, and soon they were at high romps on the grass, to my great delight. After a little more of this byplay, he began to take all sorts of liberties.

They retaliated, so that, in a quarter of an hour, the acquaintance was so far improved that they had got his breeches off and his shirt up above his waist; then Augusta falling over the root of a tree, up went her legs; he fell upon her, and then – then at it he went in good style, little Agnes behind him tickling his marbles and Augusta hugging and kissing him with all her strength.

The sight was most fucktious. His beautiful girlish bottom bounding up and down, its peach-like cheeks trembling from their very plump-ness, his stiff little cock, now in, now out; her plump thighs shining white against the greensward and her lovely shaped, hairless cunny. Add to this the various beauties her sister also displayed, and I think you will admit that a lovelier picture could not well be conceived, and I would have given fifty guineas to have had Watteau here at that moment to paint the scene.

At this enchanting moment, seeing Phoebe crossing a neighbouring copse, I called her and, putting her on all fours, engaged her as a performer in this *fête champètre*. She bounded and wriggled, I thrust; the children shouted and laughed. Sure there never was such a merry luscious scene. But as all things, even the most delightful, must have an end, and Phoebe had been very skilfully manipulating me for some minutes, amidst ah's and oh's and Oh my dear love's, and sighs and coos of delirious bliss, she died away in ecstasy. Nor were the young ones long after us. As for Augusta, she fairly ground her teeth in joy.

❧ ❧

To Helen

What an age it seems, beloved Helen, since I last saw your sylph-like form enlivening these shades. The very trees seem to droop in your absence. Cannot you come and pass a few days with us? When I think of the austere, cold-hearted man they have married you to, I feel oppressed with a sadness which no delights can dispel. Come then, my lovely Helen, and rejoice me with a view of your charms once more.

You ask me for news of our doings here; and though I have always some new adventure to relate, I should do so with more pleasure could I but identify you with this paradise.

Cecilia and I diversify our amusements. To this end she has the most cavalier servant in the world, and I two sweet girls who are entirely at my disposal.

I wish you could see Phoebe and Chloe, for you would scarcely find anywhere more lovely creatures.

Then there are my wife's little cousins, Augusta and Agnes, who come from school sometimes, and who I have initiated in all the mysteries of Venus.

Yesterday we had a garden party attended by Mrs J and three of her pupils, Mesdames Bellew, Marshall and Jennings, besides the cousins.

The sports consisted of swinging, blind-man's-buff, hunt-the-slipper, hide-and-seek, and concluded with a bath in the lake and supper on the lawn.

My new swing was hailed with acclamations by the young ladies, who with Chloe and Phoebe, not forgetting Lady Cecilia, were speedily seated therein. This filled up every seat, which relieved Mrs J, poor woman, as she had no desire, she said, to make an exhibition of herself at her age. And *entre nous*, she is a little *passé*, and has, besides, such a tremendous black bearskin in a certain quarter that the sight of so grim an affair would have spoiled the view. As for our little Daphnis (that is his *nom d'amour*, you know, otherwise he rejoices in the vulgar epithet of 'Jack'), he was in raptures and ran along the line of beauty trying to see all he could. Then, oh, the laughter, the little screams, the coquettish attempts to prevent him seeing their charms, and the badinage and saucy jokes that were bandied about, made up a scene which quite beggars description. Then as soon as the swing began to move and swung high in the air, the fun grew fast and furious and the sight was not only exciting but also most singular; for as I sat underneath, as they swung over my head, I could not see anything but bottoms, thighs, legs, and pretty little feet, all of a row. Occasionally, to obtain a firmer seat, one of them would give a wriggle or twist, which showed me some new charm – a nymphoe or clitoris would pop out – and with each movement I discovered new beauties. When they were tired of this fun, we played blind-man's-buff, I of course being blind man. The little pussies were pretty rough in their play, pushing me about at their pleasure and taking all manner of liberties; but no sooner had I caught one of them but I took my revenge, putting my hand up her clothes without ceremony. Feeling a luscious, pouting little cunny, on which a soft down was beginning to sprout, I at once recognised it and cried out, 'Ah! I know you, it is Miss Bellew.'

'Right, right!' shouted the merry voices, and pulling off the handkerchief I at once made her pay toll before them all. You will observe we went far beyond kissing here. In fact, tossing up the young lady's petticoats, I pushed her gently on her hands and knees, and having long been primed was into her in a moment. As for the others, with many a gay repartee, they seated themselves in a circle and watched the performance.

Poor Miss Bellew, as you may suppose (though nothing loth to the thing itself), would have preferred a more private place. But seeing there was no escape, she submitted with a good grace. Indeed, she need not have distressed herself, for her companions, stimulated by what they saw, were soon so fully occupied themselves as to pay little attention to us. Cecilia led Daphnis into a little grove, sacred to Priapus; Phoebe and Mrs J disappeared down an avenue; Augusta and Chloe became little tribades for the time; while the others were all frigging away right and left.

Sure the Isle of Capri in the days of Tiberius could have shown no more voluptuous scenes than those which startled the very birds in the trees from their propriety.

But, alas! this is but a terrestrial Elysium, and we soon found that we were neither gods nor goddesses. Half an hour satisfied all our desires for that bout, and all were soon seated for a game of hunt-the-slipper, which passed off with the usual pleasantries of frigging and feeling, in which I allowed Daphnis to share, and the young wag set us all in a roar by insisting that as he could not find the slipper he was sure Mrs J had put it up her cunt, and in spite of all her protestations he would feel for himself, which I have no doubt that cunning and salacious dame relished most heartily. You must know, my love, that Mrs J is still a fine woman. Ten or twelve years ago, she often had me panting on her bosom. Phew! those days are gone by; I require more juvenile stuff to give me a stiffener now.

Then came the romping game of hide-and-seek, which produced great fun. But by far the most *recherché* scene of all was the bath. You know that lovely lake, my Helen; for 'twas in its crystal water we first enjoyed love's blisses together.

In a few minutes we were all undressed and sportively splashing each other, swimming, kissing, tickling, fucking. Oh, ye gods, what a scene it was. Such perfect abandon I do verily believe was never witnessed, even at the Dionysian festivals of ancient Greece. But one thing was wanting to make us mad as the satyrs and bacchantes of those times. And that one thing I resolved to have – wine. I despatched Phoebe and Daphnis for a dozen of Burgundy. The cup circulated; we all became intoxicated; we performed prodigies of lust, gamahuched, and did everything that the most wanton imagination can conceive; so that coming at length out of the lake, in which some of the girls were near to being drowned, none of the party save Cecilia, Mrs J, and myself could dress ourselves. Calling in the aid then of old Mrs. Jukes, we first put Phoebe, Chloe and Daphnis to bed. Then, huddling on the clothes of the other young ladies, we got them, as best we might, to the coach and sent them home at seven o'clock that summer's evening, as completely drunk as ever was a lady of pleasure in Covent Garden.

As for Cecilia and myself, we partook of a light supper, went to bed, and were soon in the arms of Morpheus.

◦§◦

To Livia

I find from my excellent friend, Mrs J, that she has given you an elaborate account of our late doings here, when we emulated the ancients with our Bacchanalian orgies. The finish of that scene was not, I must confess, at all to my taste, and we all suffered more or less the next day for our excess. I have therefore determined not to proceed to such lengths again.

Yesterday, being the breaking up for the holidays at Mrs J's, I proposed to her to invite the whole school of twenty-six young ladies. But not to injure the interests of the good lady, I promised that any little amorous fun that took place should be covert and accidental, apparently.

That if any of the innocent ones saw aught that might shock their notions of propriety, it should be so managed that they would never think it was a premeditated affront.

To this end I caused the statues of Priapus to be wreathed with laurel and ivy about the middle. I locked up all the naughty books and pictures, and as it was not intended to proceed to any voluptuous extremities while the young ladies were with us, I introduced on this occasion an excellent band of musicians, who were located in a tent pitched on a spot where they could observe little of the proceedings. From Ranelagh Gardens I brought Jackson, the fireworks man, at an expense of twenty pounds. During the morning he was very busy hanging variegated lamps on both sides of every verdant valley, and the taste he displayed was wonderful. The weather continued delicious, clear and warm, so it promised to be very effective. Meantime a sumptuous refection was prepared. The new and old swing were dusted and got ready, the fountains were set a-playing, and when at three o'clock the young ladies arrived all was in readiness. Lady Cecilia looked charming in a white satin commode and quilted hoop of pink silk; her hair was delicately powdered, and Renaud, that prince of coiffeurs, had coquettishly placed a real rose on one side of her head, which had a vastly pretty effect. As for me I wore my grey tiffling coat, a pompadour waistcoat, grey satin breeches and silks, with my best pair of diamond buckles in my shoes. I also, in honour of my company, mounted my gold-hilted sword, mechlin lace ruffles, bag and solitaire.

Upon the arrival of the school we first of all discussed the viands set out on the grass under the shade of a wide-spreading elm. Six and twenty girls sitting on the lawn, you will readily suppose, could not all place themselves so correctly but what I got many a sly peep at legs, thighs, and cunnies I had never seen before; and the best of it was they were not the least aware of it, nor did the knowing ones – Mesdames Marshall, Jennings, Bellew, Augusta and Agnes – venture to give them a hint; so there I sat, eating the wing of a chicken and viewing the secret charms of four or five of the finest girls in the world.

The repast over, we proceeded to walk round the grounds, and when we came to the terminal figure of Priapus, the god of the garden, they all came to a halt; and while they considered him attentively, they asked me to explain all about his worship in ancient times, which I did to their entire satisfaction.

One tall, elegant girl of fourteen, Miss Medley, showed more curiosity than the others, and lingered behind to have a private view of the divinity. I had no doubt she wanted to see what it was the ivy concealed; so after we had got a little further I pretended that I had left my snuff box indoors, and deputing Cecilia to show them everything I stealthily returned and creeping up among the foliage at the back of the statue beheld the ivy removed and Miss Medley, on tiptoe, trying to rub her cunny against the marble Priape. Altering my position, therefore, so that she could see from my waist to my knees, but not my face, which the leaves concealed, I pulled out my own priape, which I handled till it was as big as the rural god's. She was some time before she saw it, but at length, when she did (supposing it was one of the musicians who was standing behind a tree for a necessary purpose), she re-covered the statue, and placing herself behind it peeped out to see all that she could without being seen. Of course, I shook the staff about and showed it off to the best advantage. She (not knowing I had seen her) displayed no alarm, nothing but intense curiosity; but I saw her right hand disappear under her clothes in a very mysterious manner; and from that moment I knew she was mine. With two strides I was beside her, finger on lip. She looked petrified with terror and shame, but I soon reassured her.

'My dear girl,' said I, 'this is what you want' (placing it in her hand), 'not the marble one, which is only to look at. Let me show you what use it is put to, and I promise not to tell Mrs J anything I have seen.'

'Oh, pray, good sir, what would you do? Consider my honour, my virtue. Ah, my goodness, what will become of me?'

'Why, certainly,' said I, 'it would not be very pleasant for your mamma to be told how you have acted – to have looked so long at a naked man when by quickly walking away you would scarcely have seen him. Oh, fie, miss.'

'Oh, but, Sir Charles, you will not tell, will you?'

'Certainly not, if you comply with my wishes.'

And I clasped her firm posteriors with one hand and her beautiful glowing cunny with the other.

'But, Sir Charles, will it not hurt very much?'

'Well, it will hurt a little at first, but the pleasure will soon drown the pain.'

She was silent, but I felt her hand tremble as she squeezed my great prick between her white, tapering fingers.

That was enough, so lifting her in my arms I bore her to a little grove in which was a tool house never visited by anybody but the gardeners, and here putting a bundle of matting on a turned over wheelbarrow, I deposited the fair girl and was soon driving away at her maidenhead.

She bit her lip with the pain but did not cry out, which I considered a good omen; so caressingly slapping her thighs and handling her breasts and buttocks, I soon found a sensible moisture in that luscious part into which I was forcing my way – the darling girl was spending. Soon she gave tongue in delirious ejaculation: 'Ah! where am I? Oh! how nice it is. Ah – oh – bl – bliss! Ah, oh, ur – r – r – r!'

And grinding her teeth, she nearly squeezed the breath out of me, hugging me with her arms and entwining her thighs around my loins with a tiger-like strength that nearly broke my back.

This girl, who had large open blue eyes and a confident bold air, had evidently found what she had long required, only she did not know it, and that was a good stiff cock. And having found it, she had a good mind to keep it, for my crisis having come and desiring to withdraw, she would by no means let me, but planted her touches so wantonly and with such good effect that positively (a rare thing at my time of life) I got a second erection within ten minutes of the departure of the first.

She now grew quite bold and whispered to me not to let it come so soon.

It consequently happened that we lingered half an hour in that delightful spot.

As soon as the beauteous Miss Medley had a little recovered herself, I raised her up and offered her my arm and together went in search of her companions.

'Well?' said I, 'you find the real surpasses the *beau ideal*?'

'Not the same thing at all,' she whispered, pressing my arm.

'What pains me is the reflection that just as I have won, I am to lose you. You go home tomorrow, do you not?'

'Yes, that is so,' she said; then hesitating a little, she added, 'but if you really desire it, that need not prevent your seeing me, as I live no further off than Richmond, and there are numerous lovely secluded spots where we could meet.'

I stopped involuntarily with surprise, then catching her up in my arms I covered her with kisses, exclaiming, 'Why, my angel, this is more than my fondest hopes could have suggested. Do you really mean what you say? Or, come now, acknowledge that you are laughing at me.'

'I, not the least in the world.'

'Then you really mean what you say.'

'*Ma foi*, yes; I find you a gallant man.'

I took off my hat and made a lower bow to Miss Medley than I ever made to a little miss before.

Then we pursued our conversation and she gave me full directions where I was to meet her, on what days, and at what hour. By the time she had finished we found ourselves in the midst of the merrymakers.

'Why, goodness gracious,' cried a dozen voices at once, 'where have you two been all this while? We had quite lost you both.'

Poor Miss Medley blushed, but I came to the rescue, quickly saying, 'You know, I went indoors for my snuff box; in returning I made a detour through the maze to see if the lamps had been hung to my mind and found Miss Medley, who had quite lost herself in its intricate winding and shouted to me to show her the way out, which after some time I was able to do, and here we are.'

This explanation satisfied the majority, but I saw the Misses Marshall and Jennings exchange a meaning look, which I had no difficulty in reading, but of course took no notice.

We had interrupted a capital game at hide-and-seek, which was now continued.

It being Miss Jennings' turn to hide, away she tripped into the wood, but as she passed me she managed to squeeze a little crumpled billet, written in pencil, into my hand. As soon therefore as we heard 'whoop', away we ran in every direction, and finding myself alone I seized the opportunity of reading it.

It was of a brevity perfectly Spartan: 'The tool house.'

To the tool house I therefore proceeded as fast as possible, taking care none of the huntresses should see which way I took and pondering all the way on those two words.

Had it been Miss Marshall, all would have been clear enough, but what did the little Jennings know about the tool house?

In the midst of my cogitations I saw it before me.

With a hasty glance to see that no one had followed me, I sprang over the threshold and shot the bolt behind me, and at that moment was clasped in the arms of the amorous girl.

'Oh, dear Sir Charles,' she exclaimed, 'this is kind of you, but you did awaken my passions, you know, and having aroused them, you will love me a little, will you not?'

'My darling girl,' I cried, kneeling at her feet and sliding my hands under her clothes, grasping her naked thighs, 'can you doubt it?'

'Well, yes, dear Sir Charles, I did doubt, for you are such a roué and such a votary to promiscuous love that I feared you might overlook poor little me, and now that bold Miss Medley with her great blue eyes has ensnared you – for you don't suppose your tale of the maze deceived me in the least . . .'

'Really,' said I, laughing.

'Oh, you are a terrible rake, Sir Charles.'

'You flatter me,' I said, with a low bow.

'And then,' cried the impetuous girl, as her dark eyes flashed, 'I have to contend against the charms of Lady Cecilia, and Phoebe, and little Chloe, and – '

'Stop, stop,' I exclaimed, 'and *halte la*! In these precincts sacred to Venus and Priapus the green-eyed monster Jealousy is never allowed to intrude; my love extends to beauty wherever it is to be found, and like the bee I fly from flower to flower and extract the sweets from each; be satisfied then, my precious girl, with your own share, and you will, believe me, have no cause to complain.' And I imprinted a rapturous kiss on her damask cheek.

'But we are wasting precious moments in words, *ma petite*, let us proceed to deeds, if you please.'

And suiting the action to the word, I made her kneel upon the gardener's matting, which still remained on the wheelbarrow as I had left it, and tossing up her clothes exposed her voluptuous white hemispheres.

'Oh, my; good gracious,' cried the girl, 'is that the way it is done? I thought you would lie on my bosom.'

'There are various methods, my angel,' said I, beginning to push at the mark, 'and as we become better acquainted I hope to instruct you in the thirty-five positions.'

'*Juste ciel!*' ejaculated the pretty creature, 'are there so many, then?'

'Oh, yes,' I rejoined, 'and each more delightful than the other.'

And grasping her round the hips, I began to thrust in good earnest. She buckled to admirably, and merely giving a little 'oh!' of pain now and then, straddled and aided my entrance all she could, so that in about ten minutes I rode in at a canter, winning the race by a length.

Then, as she felt the swelling head of my stiffening weapon in the innermost depths of her cunny, this enamoured girl gave full vent to her delight. She jutted out her great white bottom, she passed her hand underneath and felt the balls of love; she manipulated me in a thousand ways; she bounded, wriggled, and twisted, sighed and cooed; her breath came short, and murmuring out, 'Ah, sweet bliss! Ah, it is Heaven! Heaven!' she spent; and my ecstatic movement, by a lucky chance coming at the same time, I sank forward on those white globes in a delirium of joy.

How long we should have lain thus, Venus only knows; but the sound of approaching footsteps roused us from our voluptuous trance. Hastily arranging my dress, I slipped out of the door and hid myself amongst the underwood. I had scarcely concealed myself when a bevy of young girls appeared, shouting out at the top of their voices, 'Miss Jennings, Miss Jennings!'

'Where can she have hid herself?' cried one.

'I declare,' said another, 'I am quite hot and tired with looking for her.'

'I should not wonder if she is in this tool house,' cried another, 'let us see.'

And pushing open the door, they led her out, looking very confused and as red as a peony.

'Why, gracious goodness me, Miss Jennings, what could have induced you to choose such a place to hide?'

'Rather say,' answered the lovely girl, recovering her presence of mind, 'how foolish you all look at having been baffled so long.'

'Well, well, we have found you at last; so come along and let us have a game at hunt-the-slipper; we shall only just have time for one game before the fireworks, for see it is getting quite dark.' And the laughing girls led her off.

I was preparing to follow, not wishing to lose my share of a game I liked so well, when suddenly I felt a little hand in mine, and turning looked down on the smiling, rosy face of little Chloe.

'What! you here?' I cried, astonished. 'How's this?'

'Oh, don't be angry, your honour,' said she. 'I followed you and saw all that passed in the tool house through a chink in the door; but I will not tell.'

'Oh, you saucy little pussy,' I cried, patting her rosy cheek, 'and what do you want of me now?'

'Ah, Sir Charles, that you must guess, you know.'

'Egad,' said I, 'that I can discern quite well, you funny little thing; but tell me, do you then like to have me, better than young Daphnis. He, so young, so beautiful, so near your own age, I so old compared to yourself. Is this possible?'

'Why, to tell you the truth, Sir Charles, I have a stronger liking for you than for him. He is too pretty by half, too like a girl; besides you taught me all I know of love; you first awakened those feelings; it was your hand first caressed that secret part which now always thrills when I approach you. Oh, Sir Charles, young as I am, I have all a woman's feelings.'

'Then, my dear little love, you shall have all a woman's pleasure. Come,' and I led her into the wood, and lying on my back made her get over me.

'I am rather tired, my love,' said I, 'so you must do all the work.'

'That I will, and with pleasure, dear Sir Charles; but oh, dear me, you are not stiff, hardly at all; but I will soon remedy that. Let me gamahuche you; and if you like, do you gamahuche me and then we shall soon be ready.'

So saying, she turned round, presenting her lovely little bottom and pressing her young cunny to my lips, my tongue slipped in at once, while she, taking my languid prick in her rosy mouth, so skilfully titillated it that in a very few minutes I was ready for action.

Again, therefore, reversing her attitude, she mounted me and a delightful fuck ensued.

The whole affair did not occupy a quarter of an hour, and this little act in the drama being concluded, we joined the revels.

I will not weary you with a recapitulation of all the frolic of hunt-the-slipper; suffice it to say that without any apparent offence against propriety, I managed, accidentally as it were, to feel many a virgin cunny and many a plump thigh that night.

The fête concluded with a country dance amidst a general illumination and a superb display of fireworks. Supper was then served and my guests departed about twelve, much delighted with their visit.

When they were gone and Cecilia and I had retired to bed, we compared notes of our various adventures.

She, it appeared, had not been idle and, attaching herself to Daphnis and Miss Bellew, had retreated to the grotto where fucking and gamahuching occupied them for an hour. She had also much diverted herself with the innocence of a pretty little girl, nine-year-old Clara, to whom she had privately shown the ponies and, after exciting the young thing with the sight and by lascivious touches, had finally gamahuched and been gamahuched by to their mutual satisfaction.

She laughed heartily at the conquest I had made of Miss Medley's heart and asked if I intended to go to Richmond?

I fancied there was rather more eagerness than usual in her manner, and as I knew her not to be troubled with jealousy, I could not quite understand it. But dissembling my surprise, I answered, coolly, 'Why, yes, I suppose I must go. That girl is quite a Messalina and would never forgive me if I disappointed her.'

'Is it possible,' said Cecilia, 'her bold blue eyes meant something then?'

'Indeed they did,' I rejoined, 'and let me tell you, she is an uncommon fine girl, and quite ripe.'

Nothing more passed, and after a little languid toying, for we were both tired out, we fell asleep.

⚓

To Thalia

The following Monday was the day appointed for me to go to Richmond, but all the way, as I rode along, I felt a vague uneasiness about Cecilia which I could not account for. There was a feverish excitement of manner about her the last few days. She was absent and abstracted, gave incoherent answers, or none at all, and was altogether quite unlike herself. What could it mean? I asked myself again and again, but at length, weary of speculation, I put spurs to my horse and galloped on.

Arrived at Richmond, I put up my horse at the Star and Garter, and enquiring my way to the Rectory (as a blind) I strolled slowly on; by and by I came to the wood which Miss Medley had so carefully described to me, and following a particular path I soon arrived at the trysting place.

Imagine my surprise when, instead of my lovely friend, I found an old gypsy woman seated under the tree. On seeing me, she rose, and dropping me a curtsey handed me a little three-cornered and scented billet. I tore it open, and read these words:

I have not been sufficiently careful with my linen; some stains have been seen and my aunt will not let me go out alone – I am in despair.

I put half-a-crown into the old woman's hand and turned on my heel. She stopped me.

'What, your honour, are you going away without an effort? Consider, sir, the young lady is over head and ears in love with you; leave the matter to me, and I will arrange it.'

'Say you so, my good woman,' said I, 'in that case I will pay you well. You know who I am, I suppose?'

'Of course I do, your honour, all our tribe know you well, Sir Charles, for have you ever turned us off your land; have you ever taken us before the beak when we robbed your poultry yard; do you not let us sleep in your barns; and did you not send us camp blankets and provisions last winter? Oh, we know you very well, and a right noble gentleman you are. A little given to the girls, perhaps, like other fine gentlemen, but what of that? Now look you, Sir Charles, we gypsies have a mysterious way of finding out things – take a friendly hint, don't return the same way you came, go the other road, or blood may come of it.'

So saying, and before I could prevent her, she dived into the wood and disappeared.

The plot thickened and I began to feel now really uncomfortable, but you know cowardice was never one of my faults; besides, I had my sword, not the toy called by that name which one wears on gala occasions but a plain, strong, serviceable weapon which had served me well in several duels; I therefore rode on the way I came, regardless of the gypsy's caution.

As I rode along the road which traverses the wood skirting my demesne, I observed a coach with imperial and portmanteaus strapped upon it, drawn up as if for concealment off the road and almost hidden amongst the trees. The coachman lay stretched on the grass while the horses grazed as they stood.

Taking no further notice of this travelling equipage I rode into the wood and, tying my horse to a tree, wandered about in different directions. At length, about fifty yards from me in a small open glade, I could perceive through the trees a lady and gentleman in amorous dalliance. I approached stealthily without being seen and ensconced myself in a copse, where I had full view of all that passed, though I could not hear what was said.

On the grass lay a tall handsome dark man, who I at once recognised as Lady Cecilia's cousin, Lord William B, and lying upon the young man was her ladyship herself, her clothes thrown up, displaying all her hinder beauties which Lord B was playfully slapping as she bounded up and down upon him.

They were evidently very much pleased with each other, and the rapturous kisses, the 'oh!' and 'ahs!' were the only sounds that reached me. After some time they reversed the position, he kneeling up behind her and she wriggling and bounding in the most ecstatic delight.

At length, their climax came. She turned round and throwing her arms round her lover's neck, sank down with him quite exhausted.

In an age when the spirit of amorous intrigue pervades the court, it was not to be expected that a person of quality like Lady Cecilia would be very rigid, more especially as Lord William B was an old flame of hers.

And remembering my own infidelities towards her I should never have taken umbrage at any she might have indulged in, had they been carried on openly as mine were. But this clandestine meeting when she thought I was gone out for the day disturbed me.

I was anxious to gather from their conversation what was the meaning of it. So soon, therefore, as they had finished their first delights and were seated lovingly side by side on the grass, I crept up through the gorse and underwood till I found myself about a yard from them. Here, motionless as a statue, my hand on my sword, I listened.

'I was saying,' said Lord William, 'that this man must be a thorough old beast, a goat, a satyr, my dear coz, who ought never to have had you. The things you have told me, and pardie, I am no saint, really quite make my hair stand on end. Intrigue is one thing, damme, but to debauch children, fie, fie – '

'Perhaps,' cried Cecilia, laughing, 'he would say, could he hear you, that to amuse oneself with little children who are nobody's property is one thing, but to debauch another man's wife is another. Damme, fie, fie – '

Lord William laughed but bit his lip, annoyed at the repartee.

'In fine, my dear William,' said Cecilia, 'it is so much easier to see the wickedness of other people's actions than that of our own. I'll venture to assert that if every man now living got his deserts, there would be few would escape. Let fanatics abuse their fellow creatures, condemning them wholesale to hell – human nature, depend upon it, is the same everywhere, whether under a parson's cassock or a soldier's scarlet coat.'

'Granted, my little philosopher,' laughed her cousin, 'but did you not tell me that you regarded your husband with abhorrence and detestation?'

'Oh, doubtless, doubtless! Yes, he is detestable; a horrid, debauched old scoundrel, no question; but that is no reason you, who have just made him a cuckold, should add insult to injury by calling him names. How do you know that he is not nearer than we think and might suddenly – '

'Appear!' I hoarsely exclaimed, springing into the open space where they were seated, sword in hand. 'To your feet, my lord; draw and defend yourself. The intrigue I could have pardoned, for it is the custom of the age in which we live, but the abuse is too insulting, and on your part, my lady, too cruel; but enough of words. Guard!'

I placed myself in fencing attitude. Lord William (who was an antagonist not to be despised, being one of the first swordsmen of the day) raised his sword to his head *en salute*; then gracefully he threw himself into the second position and our blades crossed with a clashing sound that elicited a little shriek from Lady Cecilia, who sank, half fainting, on the greensward.

The duel lasted some time; we were combatants worthy of each other. *Carte* and *tierce*, *volte* and *demi volte*, all the finesse of fencing was tried by each for some time in vain.

At length I pricked him in the sword arm and his cambric sleeve was crimsoned in an instant. The wound only roused his anger; he lost his coolness and did not keep himself so well covered; lunging then under his *tierce* guard, I should certainly have despatched him had not the traitress, Lady Cecilia, at that instant struck up my arm with Lord William's cane; at the same moment his sword passed through my body. I fell back like a dead man, without sense or motion.

When I again opened my eyes, they rested on various familiar objects; I was in my private chamber. At the foot of the bed was seated Phoebe, her eyes red with weeping. I tried to speak, but she put her finger to her lip and, approaching, said, 'Pray don't try yet, Sir Charles.'

'What has happened?' I faintly exclaimed.

'Not now, not now,' whispered Phoebe; 'you shall know all about it another time. You have been light-headed and very ill, and for three days that kind young surgeon who scarcely ever left your side despaired of your life; but if you will only keep quiet, dear Sir Charles, all may yet be well.'

She put a cooling drink to my lips and, shading the light, moved further off. I found myself from loss of blood to be weak as a baby and, closing my eyes, was soon again unconscious. In another week I was a little better, to the great delight of the poor doctor (to whom I had certainly shown many acts of kindness, never expecting such a faithful and grateful return for it). He told me that the right lung had been pierced and that the haemorrhage had at first been so great that he despaired of staunching it; but that quiet, the excellent nursing of old Jukes, Phoebe and Chloe, who had sat up with me in turns, and an iron constitution had combined to save me. He said not a word of himself or his own skill, so that when, about a month afterwards, being convalescent, I presented him with a cheque for one hundred guineas, he regarded me with astonishment, declaring that ten was all he deserved;

but I would not be gainsaid and sent him away rejoicing.

Feeling myself now well enough to hear Phoebe's recital, and kissing her and Chloe and even poor old Jukes with much ardour as I thanked them for their tender care of me, I made the two former seat themselves at my feet, while Daphnis placed a pillow at my back and handed me a glass of lemonade.

'It is little I have to tell you, Sir Charles,' began Phoebe, 'but I will endeavour to be as clear as possible. Soon after your departure for Richmond, her ladyship went out alone on foot. As we had no orders to watch my lady, I would not permit Jack to do so, and we saw her no more. About five in the afternoon Jack was rambling about in the woods outside the walls when suddenly he came upon the spot where, to his great horror, you lay weltering in your blood.

'There was blood on the turf all about, which was much trampled down. You lay on your back, pale as death. Near you he picked up a fan, a ribbon and a lady's glove. Returning to the dairy at speed he at once told us what had happened, directed us to bring your body in quietly and make up a bed in this room while he galloped off for the doctor.'

'My dear boy,' said I, extending him my hand, 'your presence of mind and decision in all probability saved my life. I thank you, and will remember it. Go on, Phoebe.'

'Well, sir, we did just as he bid us, and the doctor came; you know the rest.'

'And Lady Cecilia?' I exclaimed.

'Oh,' said Phoebe, 'Jack must tell you all about her ladyship, for as soon as he had heard what the doctor had to say and saw you in good hands, he brought your horse, which you had left tied to a tree, into the yard, put a pair of loaded pistols into the holsters, buckled on your short sword and rode away.'

'Do you, then, continue the narrative, Daphnis,' said I.

The boy hesitated a moment, and then began.

'You will readily understand, Sir Charles, that being quick of apprehension, seeing you lying there with your drawn sword still in your hand, a glove, a ribbon, a fan and the prints of strange footmarks, and those, too, from shoes not such as are generally worn by the vulgar or by highwaymen, I rapidly came to the conclusion that my lady had met a gallant in the wood, that you had surprised them, and that the duel was the consequence.

'Then I followed the footprints in the moist mossy turf, which showed clear owing to the recent rains, until they nearly reached the road; here the marks of wheels appeared: a coach-and-four had been driven off the road and into the wood, had stopped where the footprints ended and then, skirting the wood, had debouched on the road. Putting spurs to your horse's flanks, I galloped on. At the next town I heard news of the fugitives; twelve miles further on they had changed horses; at the next six miles they had supped. It was now quite dark, but still I galloped on; soon however I lost them; there were three roads in diverse directions and no one could give me a clue as to the one they had taken. Horse and self being now quite worn out, I stopped at the nearest inn and retired to rest. The next morning I made the best of my way to Hastings. Here I learnt that a lady and gentleman answering their description had sailed for France five hours before.'

I thanked Daphnis for his zeal, but assured him he had taken a great deal of unnecessary trouble.

I will now conclude this long story by telling you I subsequently heard that Lord William had quarrelled with a Frenchman at a public gaming table, blows had ensued which resulted in a duel and the Frenchman had left his lordship stark dead on the field.

As for Lady Cecilia, broken-hearted at the loss of her cousin and lover, she entered a convent of Benedictine nuns and has lately taken the black veil.

But it is time to put an end to this long letter, so, adieu!

❧ ❧

CONCLUSION

To Thalia

You ask me, dear friend, where I have been hiding myself the last fifteen years. Alas! we are both that much older since we last corresponded. I was, however, about to indite a letter to you, having heard from Jack Bellsize that you had just returned from India with your husband, the General.

You duly received my communication of the affair with Lord William B, you tell me, and wrote a long letter in reply, but I never got it.

After these unfortunate events I took a disgust to my villa at Twickenham, which I sold for a good price to Sir Bulkeley H, and retreated, with Phoebe, Chloe, Daphnis and old Jukes, to my Herefordshire estate, where I have resided ever since.

As for Miss Medley, having heard from the gypsy of my intended departure she decamped one night from her aunt's and joined us. She remained with me about five years but when an opportunity arose for her to make an advantageous marriage with a young farmer, I persuaded her to have him and stocked their farm for them.

To Mrs J, I presented the house in which she lived, taking an affectionate farewell of that excellent lady. Augusta and Agnes I suitably provided for, and also found husbands for Miss Marshall and Miss Jennings, giving to each a dowry.

Poor old Jukes died five years since, come Michaelmas. Daphnis I started in life with an ensign's commission in a marching regiment when he was about eighteen; poor lad, he fell gloriously while leading his men in the forlorn hope of storming some place in the Low Countries (not Cunnyland), such are the fortunes of war; and a more gallant youth never campaigned in the fields of Venus or Mars.

Phoebe, now a fine buxom woman of thirty-five, retains all her good looks and much of her freshness. She is sweet tempered and affectionate as ever.

Chloe has grown up a lovely creature and is now twenty-eight.

Having 'lived every day of my life', as the saying is, you will readily suppose that I cannot perform the feats of Venus I once indulged in, but two or three blooming little girls who pass for the sisters and cousins of Phoebe and Chloe serve to amuse me by their playfulness, and, tumbling about showing their beauties, sometimes stir my sluggish blood into a thrill.

Occasionally I am able to remind Phoebe and Chloe of my old vigour and have a fucktious romp, but . . . 'From fifty to four-score, once a week and no more.'

They each have a strapping young fellow as a lover, and my consideration in this regard, so far from alienating them, only makes them more amiable and compliant to my wishes.

By my neighbours these dear girls and old friends are regarded as favourite domestics merely, a discreet old woman, the cook, who supplied old Jukes' place, lending propriety. So I am no longer a rake.

The rector of the parish is my very good friend.

My faithful surgeon lives in the house, being still a bachelor.

So, with the extra aid of two neighbouring squires, we have our bowl of punch and a rubber.

This quiet life suits me admirably, and I have forever bid adieu to the gay world and the pleasures of the town, passing much of my time in reading those philosophical writers who are just now making such an impression on the public mind.

And now, dear friend, having given you all the news, I would fain express a hope that you will some day find your way into this remote region, but if the fates decree otherwise, then accept my farewell. *Vale! Vale! Longum Vale!*

THE YELLOW ROOM

'There is nothing,
I am convinced by several years' experience,
so good for a girl as a thorough good flogging
administered upon her bare bottom with an
elastic birch, she having been compelled to
take off her own drawers herself.'

EXTRACT FROM A LETTER OF
MRS B. H — N

CHAPTER ONE

Simply Shocked

'*Come in,*' *said Coupeau.* '*No one will eat you!*'
L'ASSOMMOIR

When the widowed aunt of Miss Alice Darvell, with whom she had been living for several years in Yorkshire, died, her residence was transferred to her nearest relative and guardian's house in Suffolk. And the change from a small house in a bleak and lonely part of the West Riding to a baronet's establishment was hailed with rapture by the handsome and healthy girl of eighteen. The only, or at any rate, the principal, advantage gained by her life with her aunt was one she scarcely appreciated. The life, the bracing air, the country rambles, and the rigorous punctuality of the old lady had allowed Miss Darvell to develop fully the physical charms which so distinguished her. And not only that – to the fresh complexion, the laughing brown eyes, and the magnificent contours of her form and of her limbs was added a distracting air of reckless ingenuousness, picked up no doubt on her moorland scampers. But become conscious of her charms, she sighed for the pomps and vanities of the world. They were held up to her by her aunt as perils of the deadliest description – a view regarded by Alice with sceptical curiosity. Her solitude increased her imaginative faculty, and the fascination it attached to balls, parties and life generally in the world was greater than their charm actually warrants, as Alice subsequently found out. The only disquiet she had experienced arose from a vague longing which was satisfied by none of the small events in her puritanical life. She was modest even to prudishness, had long worn dresses of such a length as to make them remarkable; had never in her life had a low one on; blushed at the mention of an ankle, and would have fainted at the sight of one. The matter of sex was a perpetual puzzle to her, but she was perfectly unembarrassed in her intercourse with men, and quite unconscious of the desires she excited in them. All she knew of Sir Edward Bosmere of Bosmere Hall was that he was her trustee and guardian, that he was a widower much older than herself and a cousin some degrees removed from her; but that notwithstanding, she was to call him 'uncle'.

Thither then she went. Sir Edward turned out to be a man of about fifty; very determined in his manner, powerfully built and of a middle height. But what surprised Alice most was to find herself introduced to a tall, dark girl, who looked about two and twenty and whose name was Maud, as his housekeeper. She was dressed in exquisite fashion, but Alice thought most indecently, and she, too, called Sir Edward 'uncle'.

The first few days were taken up in making acquaintance, but Alice was surprised one morning at breakfast to see Maud grow very pale when told by Sir Edward that she was to go to the yellow room after breakfast, and that she was to go straight there. This direction was in consequence of some cutlets which were served at the meal being slightly overcooked; and when Alice again saw Maud she was flushed and excited, and appeared to have been crying her eyes out. In some consternation, she inquired what the yellow room was, and the only reply she obtained was that she would find out soon enough. On the same occasion, when Maud had left the breakfast-room, Sir Edward, who had by that time quite taken in Alice, told her he thought she dressed in a very dowdy fashion, and said he had given directions to their maid to provide a more suitable wardrobe for her. The girl was covered with blushes and confusion when he spoke of her dressing like Maud, for Maud showed a great deal of leg and glimpses too of many other charms. Alice tried to pull herself together and reply that she really could do no such thing. Sir Edward looked at her in a very peculiar way, and said he felt sure her present mode of dress hid the loveliest neck and limbs in the world. He went on to ask whether she did not admire Maud's style of dress, and if she had noticed her stockings and drawers.

'I have indeed, uncle; but I could never wear anything like them.'

'And why not, pray?'

'I should be so ashamed.'

'We will soon cure you of that. We punish prudish young women here by shortening their petticoats. How do you like the idea?'

'Not at all; and I will not have anything of the sort done to me.'

'I am afraid, miss, you want a whipping.'

'I should like' (defiantly) 'to know who would dare such a thing.'

Sir Edward again looked at her in a peculiar manner, but said nothing more on the subject. Simply observing that he thought it right that young women should learn how to manage a house before they had one of their own and did not know what to do with it, he said she and Maud were to take the management in turns weekly, and that a week from that day she would have to be housekeeper.

'In the meantime, my dear, you had better learn as much as you can from Maud; especially not to let them burn cutlets like these.' Saying which, he left the room.

At this point the narrative can best be continued by Alice Darvell herself:

Wednesday, July 3, 188–. As soon as uncle had left the breakfast-table, I felt quite disturbed, but on the whole determined to go on as if nothing had happened. A message came a little later by our maid from Maud to say that she could not go out riding as we had arranged. What a terrible woman our 'maid' is! Why on earth does uncle have a Scotch-woman of so terrible an aspect for us two girls? She makes you quake if she only looks at you. Well, I made up my mind to go alone; and rode off very soon after.

On my return I met Maud, very red, and looking as though she had been crying dreadfully. She would not tell me what had happened. The rest of the day passed in the usual way. We drove out after lunch, paid some visits, received several at our kettle-drum and dressed for dinner; while waiting for the gong to sound Maud came to me, and to my horror began talking upon precisely the same subject Sir Edward had been speaking to me about at breakfast.

'Uncle does not approve of your dresses, you little prude, and Janet' (the Scotch maid) 'has another one for you.'

'If Janet,' said I, 'has a dress for me like yours, showing my neck and breasts and back, and my feet, my ankles, my legs – I mean like yours – I declare flatly I won't wear it.'

'Don't be a fool, dear. I am mistress this week; you will be next week, as uncle has explained to you, and if you do not get rid of your ridiculous shame you will be soundly punished. You may be thankful if you are only obliged to show your legs up to your knees and your bosom down to your breasts. That is all.'

'I do not care. I have never been punished.'

'Very well,' said Maud; 'have your own way. You will soon know better.'

When I got down, there were uncle and Maud, three or four young men, and some very handsome women in low dresses, every one; I was the only one in a high dress. Uncle said something to

Maud, who whispered to me that I was to go with her. As soon as we got into the hall, she told me I was to be taken to the yellow room and that I was a goose. I asked her why; she only laughed. Arrived there, she said she was very sorry, but must obey orders. She then strapped my hands firmly behind my back. My struggles were useless in the end, but kept her so long that she said, 'I shall take care that you shall have an extra half-dozen for this.' I could not think what she meant. It got darker, and still no one came. The yellow room was in an out-of-the-way wing, and I heard the tower clock strike ten. My hands behind me began to hurt, and I began to lose my temper. I wondered how long I was to be kept there, and then who had the right to keep me; and supposed it was called the yellow room because the curtains of the windows, the valances and the bed-curtains were all yellow damask; and then I wondered what the ottoman, such an enormous one, was doing here, in company with a heavy oak table, a bar swinging from the ceiling, and – what with vexation and impatience I went to sleep.

I was awakened about half-past eleven by carriages driving off. It was pitch dark, and the curtains had been drawn. I know it was about half-past eleven because about half an hour later midnight struck. There was a footstep in the corridor, and uncle came in. He said:

'I am extremely surprised at your insubordination, miss, for which I am about to punish you.' What followed I cannot write.

So much for that part of the diary. Later on, by way of penance, Miss Alice Darvell was compelled to write out the minutest description of her punishments and her sensations and secret thoughts.

What happened was this: Sir Edward Bosmere at once informed Alice that he would have no more prudish nonsense; that he was going to strip her and flog her soundly, but that first he meant to obtain a promise from her to take off her own drawers – a very important humiliation to which to subject a proud young beauty.

She protested in the most vehement manner. He had no right to whip her; she would not be whipped by any man or anyone else; he was at once to undo her hands; being kept all the evening in that room without any dinner was quite punishment enough; she did not know why she had been punished; she would not wear horrid dresses which only served to make nakedness conspicuous; and if she was going to be treated in this way, she would go away tomorrow. As to promising to take off her own drawers, and before him, he must be mad to think of such a thing, and she would die first.

She looked lovely in her fury, and an alteration in the surface of Sir Edward's trousers showed his appreciation of her beauty. He longed to see her naked and all her charms revealed.

'I will not dispute with you, you saucy miss, and your face is too pretty to slap; I will settle accounts with your bottom – yes, your bottom, and a pretty plump white bottom I have no doubt it is. I can promise you, however, it won't be white long. Now lie across that ottoman on your face. What? you won't? Well, across my knee will do as well, and perhaps better.'

Putting his arm round her waist, he dragged the girl with him to the sofa, telling her that her shrieks and struggles in that heavily curtained and thickly carpeted room were of no avail; that even if they were heard no one would pay attention to them, and that the only result would be, if she went on, to double her punishment. He did not, however, at that moment wish to do more than examine the charms that were so jealously concealed, the magnificence of which might be easily guessed from the little that did appear of her figure. He walked her to the sofa and sat down upon it, still holding her by the waist, and then, putting her between his legs, pulled her down across his left one. Her power of resistance was very much lessened by her hands being strapped behind her, but still she managed to slide down upon her knees in front of him instead of being laid across his lap. He then held her tightly between his knees and proceded to unfasten the neck of her dress, and as the buttons were at the back he was obliged to put his arms round her and draw her so close that he felt her warm pressure upon him. The passion he felt was intensified, and the girl then, for the first time, seemed in a hazy sort of wonder as to whether the treatment she was undergoing was altogether unpleasant, which occupied her to such an extent that she ceased her useless resistance. At length the buttons were all undone to the waist. The dress was pulled down in front as far as the strapped-back arms would allow; sufficient, however, to disclose a neck as white as snow and the upper surfaces of two swelling, firm globes. Sir Edward immediately, placing his left arm under his victim's armpit and round her shoulders, drew her closer to him, spreading his legs wider, and notwithstanding her pretty cries to him to desist, inserted his right hand in her bosom. At last, succeeding in loosening her corset, he was able to caress the scarlet centre of the lovely, palpitating breast whose owner lay in most bewitching disorder in his lap. Her hair had partly fallen; her bosom was exposed by the dress three parts down and the loose corset – her eyes swam, and her colour was heightened.

'Oh, stop! uncle; oh, do, do, do stop! I never felt like this before. Whatever will become of me? I cannot bear the sensation. You have no business to pull me about so.'

'Do you not like the sensation, Alice?' asked he, stooping and putting his face into her bosom; 'and being kissed like this, and this, and this? And is not this nice?' – taking her red teat between his lips and gently playing with it with his tongue.

'Oh! uncle! whatever are you doing to me?' said the girl, flushing crimson all over, her eyes opening wide with amazement and her knees falling wider apart as she fell slightly back upon his right knee.

'Is it nice? Do you like it? Does it give you sensations anywhere else?' asked he, glancing at her waist – and then, a moment after, putting his hand down outside her dress, 'Here, for instance?'

Still a deeper blush of crimson shame, but there was a gleam of rapture after the momentary pressure, followed by the exclamation, 'How dare you?'

'How dare I, miss? We shall see. Now you will please lie on your face across my knee. You can rest on the sofa.'

'Oh, I suppose' – with some disappointment in the tone – 'that you are now going to button up my dress.'

'Am I?'

'Then what are you going to do?'

'Make you obey me, and without any more resistance, or you shall have double punishment. Lie down at once, miss.'

'Oh, uncle, don't look at my legs! Oh, do not, do not strip me. Oh, if I am to be whipped, whip my hands or shoulders; not there.'

'You are a very naughty, obstinate girl, with very much too much prudishness about you. But when you have been forced yourself to expose all you possess in the most unconcealed manner, and have been kept some days in short frocks with no drawers, there will no doubt be an improvement. And, as I said before, I shall flog your bare bottom soundly, Miss Alice; and pretty often if you do not mend. Lash your arms and shoulders, indeed. I shall lash your legs and thighs. Lie down this instant.'

The poor girl, seeing resistance useless, said nothing; but the arm put round her back soon cured her inaction. She lay across her uncle's left leg and under his left arm, which he had well round her waist.

'Now,' said he, tightening his grasp, 'we shall see what we have all along so carefully hidden, eh, miss?' and he pulled up her dress behind, despite her struggles and reiterated prayers to him to desist.

'No use struggling, miss,' he went on, slipping his hand up her legs and proceeding at once to that organ in front which woman delights to have touched.

'Oh, uncle! oh, leave off. How dare you? How dare you outrage me like this? Oh! take your hand away! Oh! oh! oh!'

'So you are a little wet,' feeling the hairs moistened by the voluptuous sensations he had caused her by caressing her breasts; 'and you hoped that no one would know, no doubt. Now just let me stroke these legs. What a nice' (turning the robe above her waist) 'fine pair they are; and' (opening the drawers) 'what a pretty, what a perfectly lovely bottom! What a crime to hide it from me. However, you will make amends for that by taking your drawers off presently.'

'Never! never while I live! You monster! you wretch! If ever I get out of this room alive I will expose you!'

'My dear, let me try a little gentle persuasion, a novel sensation. If that does not suffice, I can find some more striking argument.'

And, again pressing her down upon him, he slipped his hand up, and putting his finger in her virgin orifice in front, he placed his thumb in the rear. Feeling his finger first, she jerked herself upwards, upon which in went his thumb; then, with a little scream, again bouncing forwards, his finger slid in as far as her maidenhead would admit – her hands were all the time still tied. He kept up a severe use of both his finger and thumb for some moments so that she was unable to contain herself and was ultimately obliged to abandon herself to the sensations he provoked. Her legs were stretched out and wide apart; her bottom rose and fell regularly; her lovely neck and shoulders, which were still exposed to his sight, increased his rapture and, at it, her dismay; and at last, when the crisis arrived – pretty nearly at the same moment did it overtake them both – she lay panting and sobbing, almost dead with shame; but for the time subdued.

'Well, dear, how do you like your new experience?'

'Oh, uncle, it is awful, simply awful! I am beside myself.'

'When you have rested a moment, will you stand up and take off your drawers before me?'

No answer.

'Answer directly, miss.'

With a sudden revulsion of feeling, she bounced out: 'No; I won't! I won't, and you shall not.'

Getting up, he went to a chest of drawers, and, opening a drawer, took out a riding-whip. Silently, and notwithstanding her violent resistance, he again got the refractory girl over his knee, with his arm round her, her dress up, and her bottom as bare as her drawers would admit. Across the linen and the bare part he gave her a vigorous cut, making the whip whistle through the air. It fell, leaving a livid mark across the delicate white flesh, and caused a yell of pain. Again he raised it and brought it down – another yell and desperate contortions.

'Oh, uncle, don't! Oh! no more! no more! Oh! I can't bear it. I will be good. I will obey.'

Sir Edward paid no attention, and raising the whip, made it whistle a third time through the air. A more piercing shriek.

'It is not enough for you to promise to obey; you must be punished, and cured of your obstinacy. And you called me a wretch and monster' – swish – swish – swish.

'Oh! oh! oh! oh! oh! oh! oh! don't! oh! don't! Oh, you are not! I say you are not anything but what – oh! oh! put down that whip. Oh! please, dear uncle! You are not a wretch! or monster! I was very naughty to call you so, and I liked what you did to me, only was ashamed to say it. I will take my drawers off before you, if you like! I will do *anything*, only don't whip me any more.'

'You shall have your dozen, miss' – swish. 'So you liked my tickling your clitoris, did you, better than' – swish – 'tickling your bottom with this whip, eh?' – swish – swish. 'You will expose me if you escape alive, will you?' – swish – swish.

'Oh, stop, stop! You have given me thirteen. For heaven's sake, stop!'

'I have given you a baker's dozen, and' – swish – 'there is another because you complained.'

Sir Edward was carried away by the passions excited by punishing this lovely girl, and her yell as the whip again cut into her delicate flesh he did not hear, so beside himself was he. Still holding her, he asked the sobbing girl whether she would be good.

'Yes. Indeed, indeed I will.'

'There is a very satisfactory magic in this wand. Now, if I unfasten your hands, will you stand up and take your drawers off so that I may birch your bottom for refusing to wear a proper evening dress?'

'Oh, uncle, you have whipped me once, and punished me severely, too, by what you did to me. Why should I be put to more shame?'

'Shame! Nonsense. You should be proud of your charms and glad to show them. What I did should give you pleasure. Anyhow, will you take off your drawers?'

'Oh!' (flushing and in despair) 'however can I? I should have to lift my dress quite up, and I should be all exposed. Besides, it is so humiliating.'

'Precisely – you yourself must bare all your hidden fascinations. And the humiliation is to chastise your prudishness. You must do it. You had much better be a good, obedient girl, as you promised you would be just now.'

'Very well. I will then.'

'That is a good girl. You shall have a kiss for reward,' and, putting his lips on her beautiful mouth, Sir Edward gave her a long and thrilling kiss, inserting his tongue until it came into contact with hers.

'What a delicious kiss,' she said, shuddering with delight; and coyly added: 'I shall not so much mind taking off my – my – my drawers' (in a hushed tone, her eyes averted from him) '*now.*'

'That is right, dear. Now let me undo your hands. There. Now stand before that mirror and let me arrange the light so that it may fall full upon you. Now I shall sit here.'

Miss Alice Darvell walked over to the mirror in a graceful and stately fashion, and started as she saw herself. She turned round and looked shyly at her master, but said nothing. Stooping down, she gathered up her gown and petticoats in her arms and slowly lifted them to her waist. The act revealed a slender and graceful pair of ankles and calves, but the knees were hidden by the garment she was about to remove. After some fumbling with the buttons about her waist – they increased her confusion by not readily unbuttoning, at which she, in a charming little rage, stamped angrily once or twice – the drawers tumbled down.

'Keep up your petticoats,' cried Sir Edward, 'and step out of your drawers. Keep them up,' said he, rising, 'until I tell you you may let them down. What lovely thighs! what splendid hips! what a lovely, soft, round bottom! Look at it, Alice, in the glass.'

'Oh,' she said, simply, 'I am so glad you think so. I have never looked at myself before.'

At which he laughed, and stroked the satin skin with his hand, rubbing her limbs in front and behind and all over her bottom, until at last, when he had gradually stroked her all the way up, he put his hand between the cheeks of her back right through to her cunt, which, and the passage also, he kept gently stroking for some minutes, while she rested against him, uttering inarticulate sounds of delight.

'There,' he said at length, 'that will do for tonight. You may let your clothes down now. It is so late that the birching shall be postponed until the morning.'

'May I take my drawers with me?'

'No, my dear; it will be some time before I shall allow you to wear them again.'

'Oh, uncle!'

'Not as long as you are a maiden,' added he, significantly.

'Oh, that will be years.'

'Will it?' he inquired, innocently.

'Come,' he went on, 'I will take you to your room. You will in future occupy that one to which I am now going to take you, and not your old one.'

'Why, uncle? All my things are in the old one.'

'That does not matter, my dear. I must keep you under my eye until you are reduced to abject submission.'

The room to which he took her was cheery and warm. Although the month was July, a fire had been lighted, and had evidently been recently stirred. And on a small table near the hearth stood a biscuit box and a small bottle of Dry Monopole. Alice would have preferred a sweeter wine, but was told that was better for her. It was quite plain that either uncle had told someone the precise hour at which he would bring her to the room, or that someone had been watching, for the wine was still frothing in the glass, and therefore must have been poured out but the moment before she entered. Terrible thought – could anyone have been watching *her* and have seen her nakedness? Her uncle could not have known at what hour he would take her there. She was for an instant paralysed at the notion; but the next moment, accidentally catching sight of a bare breast and arm, she felt a certain voluptuous thrill to think she may have been seen by someone besides Sir Edward. As she slowly undressed herself, her uncle having gone off and shut the door behind him, it struck her that she would herself, for her own satisfaction, have a peep at all she had been compelled to expose to him. She blushed at her own resolution, and commenced to feel what Miss Rosa Broughton describes as delightfully immoral – a sensation, first taught her by her uncle's hands, of which all her lifetime until then she had been wholly ignorant, although she had had at times a conviction that some such pleasure existed. She stood before one of the large glasses with several of which her room was furnished, and having let down her wealth of brown hair and divested herself of all but a single garment, she allowed that – her chemise – to slip off her shoulders and arms, and for an instant only gazed at herself in the glass. For an instant only, for, overcome by a flood of shame at her nakedness and at the sense of it, she hurriedly averted her eyes and looked about her for her nightdress. But this she could not find; and she then recollected that the room was not the same she had previously used, and supposed they must have forgotten to bring her things. No; here was her dressing-gown. She would put it on, and go to her old room for her nightdress.

She went to the door, and to her utter amazement found that there was no handle inside. She was a prisoner. She looked about, but there was no other door anywhere to be seen.

'Very well,' she said to herself; 'I shall have to sleep in my chemise.'

Being naked once more in taking off her dressing-gown to put on the chemise again made her feel immodest, and as the chemise was cut low in the neck and left her arms bare, she felt more immodest still when she had got it on – a sensation renewed on several occasions when she awoke during the night and was reminded by her bare arms of her plight and of what she had undergone – and was to undergo later in the morning.

Before she got into bed she looked about for the article ladies generally use. There was nothing of the kind in the room, and there was no bell. Then it struck her that the confiscation of her nightdress and of the utensil referred to must have been done deliberately by Sir Edward, and the idea that he had thought of such things so intimately connected with her person gave her a fresh delightful glow of sensuality as she plunged into the cold, silky, linen sheets. The necessary effort to retain her urine, the sense that she was being punished by being made to retain it, and the knowledge that her uncle knew all about it and was so punishing her, excited her to such an extent that she went to bed a very naughty girl indeed.

CHAPTER TWO

Initiation

'Don't be afraid; a little bleeding does 'em good.'

L'ASSOMMOIR

Awaking next morning about nine o'clock, she caught herself wondering what the whipping would be like, and how it would be administered, and was filled with a delightful sense of shame when she recollected the part of her body which would receive the castigation and the exposure it would inevitably entail. The thought or anticipation of this did not disturb her much. She even contemplated with pleasure the exposure there would be of her legs and thighs, and of that which she did not name to herself, considering the word immodest; but she did trust that her uncle would not flog her very severely.

As she lay thus occupied with these thought there was a tap at the door, and Janet came in with a cup of tea and some bread and butter and the announcement: 'You have just an hour for dressing, miss, for breakfast will be served at half-past ten in the blue sitting-room – the one which overlooks the park. Miss Maud will come to show you where it is.'

'Thank you, Janet,' said Alice, keeping herself carefully covered. 'There are several things I want from my old room – linen and a dress. Will you please bring them?'

'Yes, miss. I have the clothes you are to wear all ready, and will bring them to you.'

'What do you mean, Janet?'

Janet did not reply. She grimly thought she would leave the girl to find out for herself.

She returned presently with an armful of clothing, which she deposited on a sofa.

In the meantime Alice had jumped up and donned the dressing-gown. She then again found it necessary to look about for that piece of furniture which is a feature in most bedrooms, but could not find it anywhere. She did not know, however, how to mention the matter to Janet, and while she was wondering how to accomplish it, that amiable domestic had left the room. Alice had told her to return in about half an hour to do her hair, and the reply was that her hair was not to be done up that morning – a circumstance which, recalling what was before her, made her blush deeply. Then Janet departed, shutting the door, which only opened from the outside. Alice, consoling herself with the reflection that she could wait at any rate until she was on the way to breakfast, proceeded to wash. In the wall, close to the wash-hand-stand, was a black marble knob, with the word 'Bath' upon it in gold letters. It was exactly what she wanted at the moment. Putting her hand upon it, she happened to press slightly, whereupon the panel slid aside and showed a marble-floored room surrounded by looking-glasses, with several large slabs of cork for standing on, and a large bath of green Irish marble in the centre. Proceeding to it, she found that the same mechanism filled the bath with water as opened the room itself. She soon ascertained that not only was the water perfumed, but deliciously softened. The champagne and the tea made her wish again that she could have got rid of the water she herself contained, but she could not make out how the water ran away or was made to run away from the bath – so that little idea was knocked on the head. While bathing, she caught sight of herself continually in the glasses about her, and fell in love with her round, plump limbs and frame, and wondered why she had never done so before. She also noticed with indignation the red marks across her bottom made by the cruel whip the night before, and shuddered as she dried herself with the deliciously woolly and warmed towels and remembered that she had a flogging to undergo. She came, however, to the conclusion that her disobedience deserved punishment; she felt naughty, and she confessed to herself that she 'really deserved to be whipped for it'.

Hardly had she so determined than she found her obedience again put to the test. Proceeding to dress, she found the clothes brought far worse than the dress she had refused to wear the evening before. They were fit for a girl of ten, and, indeed, unfit for even her. The chemise was abominably low behind and before, the petticoats were quite short. So was the dress. And the petticoats were so starched that instead of hiding her limbs they would display them. And there were no drawers. What was she to do? Sir Edward was rigid in exacting punctuality at meals and generally. If she waited till Maud came she would be too late, and probably receive a worse flogging; besides, in all probability, Maud would only again laugh at her. So, a little indignantly, she dressed herself in the white silk stockings, which reached just half-way up her thigh, tied them with the rose-coloured garters above her knee, put on the patent leather low-cut shoes, the black and yellow corset, and the white frock with the rose-coloured sash. She tied her hair with a ribbon of the same colour, and then looked at herself. She looked like a great, overgrown schoolgirl, but, she could not help owning to herself, a very lovely one. Her arms were bare, and the frock was so low that she noticed with horror it only just concealed her red teats; at least, looking at her from straight in front, it did, but if you looked down from her shoulder they were quite visible. And the dress stopped at her knees; no effort could make it longer. And the petticoats would make it stick out so. The only comfort was her hair, which did help to hide her naked back. Dressed at last, but feeling worse than naked, she sat down to wait for Maud, and, to her horror, noticed in a glass opposite that the dress stuck out to such an extent that not only could her leg be seen to the top of the stocking, but the rosy flesh beyond was quite visible; and after a trial or two she discovered that if she was not very careful how she sat, not only would the whole of both legs be displayed, but her cunt also. She wondered however she could go about like this, and whether she would have to; and at last the costume so excited her passions that she was compelled to walk up and down, and became so naughty that she did not know how to contain herself or the water she had been unable to get rid of.

While she was fidgeting about the room in this state of agitation, Maud entered, and immediately exclaimed, in the most disingenuous manner, 'How perfectly lovely you are, Alice, with that blush-rose flush! What a splendid bust! Good gracious! do let me look at them. What lovely straight beautifully-shaped legs' (catching hold of the skirt of the frock). 'Oh, do let me see – '

'Oh! don't, Maud! Don't!'

'Very well, dear. But you have not done up your hair. That won't do.'

'Janet told me I was not to.'

'Yes; I know. But that was a mistake. It hides too much.'

'That is just why I like it down.'

'And just why I do not, dear. You must let me roll it up for you so that your back and nuque and shoulders may be fully shown. There, now you look a perfect darling. I thought I should find you quite cured of your anxiety to hide every charm. Do you not wish now you had taken my advice?'

'Yes.'

'But,' she went on, 'it is not of much consequence; for if you had not rebelled, some other excuse would have been made for punishing you.'

'Indeed?'

'Yes; and you deserved it, Alice.'

As Alice had herself come to this conclusion, and felt her bare legs, she only blushed, and said: 'Oh, Maud, do you know I have no drawers on; and that when I sit down my legs and all show? Shall I have to go about in this dress? and how long shall I have to wear it?'

'That depends upon how you take your punishment. While you wear it you will certainly have to go about in the house and grounds with it. I suppose you wish you had drawers on?'

'Indeed you may suppose so. Oh, Maud, however can I – '

'We must be going, Alice, or we shall be late.'

'Oh, Maud, do tell me, does uncle whip very hard?'

'I should have thought,' and Maud's eyes flashed, 'you could have answered that question yourself.'

'Yes. He hurt me dreadfully with the riding-whip. Have you been birched?'

'Yes. I have.'

'Was it very bad?'

'In a few hours you will be able to judge for yourself.'

'How does he birch?'

'Here,' said Maud, slyly putting her hand under Alice's petticoats upon her bare bottom.

'Oh, don't, Maud.'

'Silly child, you should be obliged to me for the sensation. Do come along to breakfast.'

'Oh, Maud, there is something I want to ask you; but how to do it I do not know. Perhaps' (with a deep blush) 'the best way is to say they have forgotten to put something in my room.'

'I know very well what you mean, Alice. You mean you have no po; and you want to pee. All I can say is that I hope you do not want to very badly, because it is not at all likely that you will be allowed to do so until after your flogging. But, of course, you can ask uncle.'

'However could I ask him?' replied Alice, aghast and pale at the notion and the prospect of what she would have to endure. 'Does he know?' remembering her thought of the night.

'Yes. Of course he knows; and he does it to punish you, and to help to make you feel naughty. Do you feel naughty, dear?' asked Maud, and, again putting her hand under Alice's petticoats, she began tickling her clitoris.

'Oh, don't! Maud. Oh, pray don't! Oh, you will make me wet myself if you do. Oh, can't you let me go to your room?'

'My dear girl, if I were to let you pee without permission, I should probably be forbidden to do so oftener than twice in the twenty-four hours for a week or a fortnight. And I advise you to say nothing about it to uncle, for if he finds out that you want to very badly, he will probably make you wait another hour. It is a very favourite punishment of his.'

'Why?'

'Oh, I don't know; except that it is a severe one. And it is awfully humiliating to a girl to have to ask; but it certainly makes one feel naughty.'

'Yes; it does. Do you know, I was nearly doing it in the bath?'

'Lucky for you that you did not. It would certainly have been found out, and you would have caught it. But, Alice, why do you say "doing it" instead of "peeing"? When you ask you will have to use plain language.'

'Oh, Maud!'

'Yes; and very likely have to do it before uncle. If he finds out you squirm about saying things and calling them by their names, he will make you say the most outrageous things, and write them also. But there is half-past ten chiming. Come along.'

When they got to the blue room – on the way to which they passed, to Alice's intense consternation, several servants who gazed impassively at her – they found Sir Edward there in a velvet coat and kilt. He greeted them cheerily. The view across the park, in the glades of which the fallow deer could be seen grazing, was lovely; the sunshine was flooding the room, and the soft, warm summer air wafted in the perfume of the flowers from the beds below (the blue room was on the bedroom floor) through the windows, which were thrown wide open. Alice was so struck by the view that for a moment she neglected to notice how her uncle was gazing at her – but then she felt the air on her legs, and it provoked a consciousness at which she blushed.

'How do you like your frock, my dear? It becomes you admirably.'

'Does it, uncle?' Looking coyly at him. 'I am glad you like it.'

'I am glad to see you are a sensible girl after all. We shall make something of you.'

'How long am I to wear it, uncle?'

'For a week.'

'For a fortnight,' struck in Maud, maliciously. 'She is to be mistress next week.'

Maud knew very well she would find it much worse to be dressed like that when giving orders, and that her orders would not be so well attended to. She revelled in the notion of getting Alice soundly punished.

Sir Edward noticed with a gleam of amusement how fidgety Alice became towards the end of the meal, and Maud smiled gently to herself. Alice thought that after breakfast she would have a chance. She was disappointed. Sir Edward then said, in a severe tone: 'I think, Miss Alice, we have a little business to settle together. Your disobedience cannot be overlooked. You must come with me. Your short skirts will punish your prudishness, but the birch is the best corrector of a bold, disobedient girl's bottom,' She grew quite pale, and trembled all over, both with fright and at being spoken to so before Maud, who, reposing calmly in her chair, was steadily gazing at her.

She had got up. When her uncle had finished speaking, he came up to her and took hold of her left ear with his right hand, and saying, 'Come along, miss, to be flogged,' marched her off to the yellow room.

There, to her consternation, she saw straps and pillows on the oak table. In a perfect fright, she said: 'Oh, pray do not strap me down, uncle; pray do not. I will submit.'

'Undress yourself,' he said, having closed the door; 'leave on your stockings only.'

'Oh, uncle!'

'You had better obey, miss, or you shall have a double dose. Take off your frock this instant . . . Now your petticoat bodice . . . Now your petticoats . . . Now your corset and chemise. Now, my proud young beauty, how do you feel?'

He had not seen her to such advantage the evening before. She had then had her long dress on the whole time, and while punishing her he had only uncovered a small portion of her legs. It is true she afterwards had been made to take off her drawers; but the skirt and petticoats gathered about her hips had still concealed much. Now she was naked from the crown of her head to her rose-coloured garters. Burning with shame, she put her hands up to her face, and remained standing and silent while Sir Edward feasted his eyes upon every exquisite detail of the lovely little head poised so beautifully upon the perfect throat; of the dimpled back and beautifully rounded shoulders; of the arms, of the breasts and hips and thighs. It was the most lovely girl he had seen, he said to himself, and then, seating himself, he commanded out loud: 'Come here, miss. Kneel down: there, between my knees. Clasp your hands, and say after me:

'Uncle, I have been . . . '

' "Uncle, I have been . . . " '

'A naughty, disobedient girl . . . '

' "A naughty, disobedient girl . . . " '

'And deserve to be soundly birched.'

' "And deserve to be soundly birched." '

'Please, therefore . . . '

' "Please, therefore . . . " '

'Strap me down . . . '

'Oh, no! oh, no! Oh, please don't strap me down!'

'Say what I tell you at once, miss, or it will be the worse for you.'

' "Strap me down . . . " '

'To the table . . . '

'Oh! oh! oh! "To the table . . . " '

'With my legs well apart . . . '

'Oh, dear! I can't. "With – with – " I can't – "with my – " oh, uncle!'

'An extra half-dozen for this.'

'Oh, uncle!'

'Say at once: With my legs well apart.'

' "With my – my – " oh! – " legs" ' (and she shuddered deliciously and blushed bewilderingly) ' "well apart." '

'And give me . . . '

' "And give me . . . " '

'Please . . . '

' "Please . . . " '

'Four and a half dozen . . . '

'Oh, uncle! please not so much!' (recollecting the baker's dozen with the riding-whip).

'You will have more if you do not say it at once.'

' "Four and a half dozen . . . " '

'On my bare bottom.'

'Oh! that! – my – I can never say – '

'*You must.*'

' "My bare – " '

'You had better say it. Stop; I will improve it. You must say: "On my girl's bare bottom." '

'Oh, uncle!' she said, looking at him; and seeing his eyes gloating upon her and devouring her beauty, and the lust and fire in them, she immediately turned hers away.

'Now, Alice, "On my girl's bare bottom." '

' "On my girl's bare bottom." '

He moved as he said this, and Alice noticed he adjusted something under his kilt.

'Well laid on.'

' "Well laid on." '

'Yes; I will, my dear. I will warm your bottom for you as well as ever any girl ever had her bottom warmed. I will set it on fire for you. You will curse the moment you were disobedient. I will cure you of disobedience and all your silly nonsense. Come along to the table. There, stand at that end' – Alice began to sob – 'put the cushion before you, so. Now lie over it, right down on the table. No resistance' (as he fixed the strap round her shoulders she made a slight attempt at remonstrance). The strap went round her and the table, and when once it was buckled she could not, of course, get up. He then buckled on two wristlets, and with two other straps fastened her wrists to the right and left legs of the table, then another broad strap was put round the table and the small of her back. This was pretty tight, as were also those that at the knees and ankles fastened her legs, wide apart, to the legs of the table. She was like a spread eagle, and her bottom, the tender skin between its cheeks, her cunt, and her legs were most completely exposed.

'Now, my dear, you will remain in that position half an hour and contemplate your offences, and then you shall have as sound a flogging as I ever gave a girl.'

'Oh, uncle, before you flog me, do let me do something. Maud told me I should have to tell you, but I do not know how to. I will come back directly and be strapped down again if you will only let me. And, oh! please do not leave me in this dreadful position for half an hour.'

'You must say what it is that you want.'

'Oh, uncle' – feeling it was neck or nothing – 'do let me go and pee before I am flogged. I want to, oh, so dreadfully. I have not been able to all the morning, nor all night.'

'So you want to very dreadfully, do you, miss?' and going up to her he put his hand between her legs from behind, and severely tickled the opening through which the stream was burning to rush. It was all that Alice could do to retain it.

'Oh, don't! Oh! If you do I shall wet myself. I shall not be able to help it. Oh, uncle, pray, pray don't! Oh, pray let me go!'

'No, miss, I certainly shall not. It is a part of your punishment. There was an unnatural coldness about these parts of yours which this will help to warm up. Have you not felt more naughty since you have had all that hot water inside you? And are you beginning to see how ridiculous prudishness is? Now, just you think about your conduct and your disobedience until I return to whip you, and remember you owe your present shameful position to them.'

Saying this, Sir Edward left the room. Poor Alice, left to herself – all naked save for her stockings; her arms stretched out above her head and tightly strapped; her legs divided and fastened wide apart; the most secret portions of her frame made the most conspicuous in order that they might be punished by a man – did feel her position acutely. She considered it and felt it to be most shameful. Her cheeks burned with a hot, red glow. But all concealment was absolutely impossible; the haughty beauty felt herself prostrate before, and at the mercy of, her master, and experienced again an exquisite sensual thrill at the thought that she really deserved to have her bottom whipped by her uncle.

Presently Maud came into the room in a low-necked dress, with a large bouquet.

'Well, Alice,' she said, 'I hope you enjoy your position and the prospect before you.'

'Oh, Maud; go away. I can't bear you to see me in this position. I won't be punished before you.'

'Silly goose! Young ladies strapped down naked, and stretched out for punishment like spread eagles, are not entitled to say shall or shan't. What a lovely skin and back, Alice. Alas! before long that pretty, plump, white bottom will present a very altered appearance. How many are you to have?'

'I was made to ask for four dozen and a half, well laid on.'

'And you may depend upon it, you will have them, my dear, most mercilessly laid on' – stroking her legs and thighs, which caused Alice to catch her breath and to coo in a murmuring way from the pleasure Maud's hand gave her. Maud asked her whether she had tried to induce her uncle to let her go somewhere.

'Yes,' replied Alice; 'I did. But he would not.'

'And I suppose you want to very badly,' went on Maud, maliciously placing her fingers on the very spot.

'Yes; I do. Oh, don't, Maud, or you'll make me!'

'Now mind, Alice, whatever you do, hold out till your birching is over. If you do not I warn you that you will catch it.'

'I think it is a very, very cruel, horrid punishment,' said Alice, whimpering.

'It is severe, I know, and it is far better not to be prudish than to incur it. But here comes uncle.'

'Now, you bold, disobedient girl, I hope you feel ashamed of yourself,' said Sir Edward, entering the room and shutting the door. 'Maud will witness your punishment as a warning to her what she will receive if she is disobedient.'

Going up to the wardrobe, he selected three well-pickled birches, which had evidently never been used, for there were numbers of buds on them. They were elastic and well spread, and made a most ominous switching sound as, one by one, Sir Edward switched them through the air at which Alice shuddered and Maud's eyes gleamed.

'Oh, pray, pray, uncle, do not be very severe. Remember it is almost my first whipping. It is awful!'

Maud had changed the dress she had worn at breakfast and, as already mentioned, now had on one cut very low in the body; her arms were bare and her skirts short. Between her breasts was placed a bouquet of roses.

'Hold these,' said Sir Edward, giving her the rods.

He then put his left arm round Alice, and said: 'Now, you saucy, disobedient miss, your bottom will expiate your offences, and by way of preface' – smack, smack with his right hand, smack, smack, smack. 'Ah, it is already becoming a little rosy.'

'Oh, uncle! Oh, how you hurt! Oh, how your hand stings! Oh! oh! oh!'

'Yes. A bold girl's bottom must be well stung. It teaches her obedience and submission' – smack – 'what a lovely, soft bottom!' – smack, smack, smack.

Maud's eyes gleamed and her face flushed, as Alice, wriggling about as much as the straps allowed, cried softly to herself. When her uncle had warmed her sufficiently, he removed his arm and moved about two feet away from the girl – whose confusion at the invasion of her charms by the rough hand of a man increased her loveliness tenfold. Maud held one birch in her right hand. She, too, looked divine. Her dark eyes flashing, her lovely bosom heaving, she handed it, retaining the other two in her left hand, to her uncle. Alice could not see that as she gave him the birch, as soon as her hand was free she slipped it under her uncle's kilt from the back, and the instant increase of his passion and excitement left no doubt as to the use she was making of it. Sir Edward stood at the left side of his refractory ward. He drew the birch, lecturing her as he did so, three or four times upwards and downwards from back to front and from front to back between the cheeks of the girl's bottom, producing a voluptuous movement of the lovely thighs and little exclamations of delight.

'Oh! oh! oh! don't do that! Oh! oh! how dreadful! Oh, please uncle!' trying to turn round, which, of course, the straps prevented. He next proceeded to birch her gently all over the area, the strokes increasing in vigour, but being always confined to the bottom.

'Oh, uncle, you hurt! Oh! how the horrid thing stings! Oh! it is worse than your hand! Oh! stop! Have I not had enough?'

'We will begin now, miss,' said he, having given her a cut severe enough to provoke a slight cry of real pain, 'and Maud will count.'

Lifting up the rod at right angles to the table on which she was bound down, he brought it down with a tremendous swish through the air across the upper parts of her hips.

'One,' said the mellow voice of Maud – her right hand and a portion of her arm hidden under her uncle's kilt, the movements of its muscles under the delicate skin and the wriggles of the Baronet showing that Maud had hold of and was kneading a sensitive portion of his frame. The bottom grew crimson where the stroke had fallen, and the culprit emitted a yell and gasped for breath. With the regularity of a steam-hammer, he again raised the rod well above his shoulder, and again making it whistle through the air, he again gave her a very severe stroke.

'Two,' said Maud quietly.

A shriek. 'Oh! stop! Oh! stop! Oh! *stop!*'

Swish. 'Three,' calmly observed Maud.

'Oh! you will kill me. *Oh!* I can't – I can't – '

Swish. 'Four, uncle.'

'Oh, ah! Oh, I can't bear it! Oh, I will be good! Oh, Maud, ask him to stop – '

Swish. 'Five'

Maud had given her uncle an extra pull when Alice had appealed to her, and this stroke was harder in consequence. Spots of blood began to appear where the ends of the birch and its buds fell, especially on the outside of the off thigh. The yell which followed number five was more piercing, and choking sobs ensued; but Sir Edward, merely observing that she would run a very good chance of extra punishment if she made so much noise, without heeding her tears or contortions or choking, mercilessly and relentlessly gave her six, seven, eight and nine, each being counted by Maud's clear gentle voice.

'Now miss, that you have had one-sixth of your punishment – '

'One-sixth! Oh! oh! oh! I can't bear more! Oh, I can't bear more! Oh, let me off! You will kill me! Oh, let me off! I will – I will, I *will* indeed be good – '

'I suppose you begin to regret your disobedience.'

'Oh, don't punish me any more,' cried the girl, wriggling and struggling to get free – of course ineffectually, but looking perfectly lovely in her pain.

'Yes! You must receive the whole number. It is not enough to promise to obey now; you should have thought of this before. You are now having your bottom punished, not only to make you better in future, but for your past offences.'

And Sir Edward walked round to the right side of his niece, and there, in the same place, but from right to left, gave her nine very severe cuts. Alice yelled and screamed and roared and rolled about as much as she possibly could, perfectly reckless as to what she showed.

The next nine were given lengthwise between her legs. Her bottom being well up, and the legs well apart, the strokes fell upon the tender skin between them, and the long, lithe ends of the rod curled round her cunt, causing her excruciating agony.

'There is nothing like a good birching for a girl.' Swish.

'One,' said Maud, moving voluptuously.

'Oh! oh! yah! Oh! my bottom! Oh! my legs! Oh! how it hurts! Oh! oh! oh!'

'They are all the better for the pain!' Swish.

'Two,' said Maud.

'Oh! oh! oh! Oh, don't strike me there!' as the birch curled round her cunt.

'And the exposure. I do not think you will disobey.' Swish.

'Three,' said Maud, apparently beside herself, her eyes swimming.

'Oh! oh! oh! yah! Oh! I shall die! I shall *faint*! Oh! dear uncle! I will – please forgive me – I will never disobey. I will do *anything*; ANYTHING; ANYTHING!'

'I dare say you will, miss; but I shall not let you off,' – swish – 'there's another for your cunt.'

'Four,' said Maud.

'Oh! Oh! not there! Oh! I am beside myself! I shall go *mad*! I shall *die* or go *mad*!'

'You will not do anything of the sort, and you must bear your punishment.' Swish.

'Five,' counted Maud.

The cries gradually lessened, and the culprit seemed to become entranced, whereupon the uncle, at whom Maud looked significantly, directed the remaining four strokes to the insides of the thighs, leaving the palpitating red rose between them free from further blows, *for the present.*

Alice's moans were then succeeded by piercing shrieks, but her uncle, perfectly deaf to them, continued the flogging. When the third nine, given lengthwise, had been completed, Sir Edward put down the birch he had used and took a second from Maud. During the pause, his niece, with sobs and tears, earnestly implored him to let her off. For all reply, he again took up his station at her left side, and – saying: 'No, miss; I shall certainly not unstrap you; you have been far too naughty. I will punish you, and your lovely legs and bottom, to the fullest extent of the sentence, and teach you to be good, you bold hussey, and give you a lesson you will not forget in a hurry' – gave her nine more sound cuts; but this time, instead of their being administered on the upper part of her bottom, perpendicularly, they were given almost horizontally on its lower part, where it joins the thigh. Fresh yells and shrieks, all of no avail, were uttered by the unhappy girl, who in her agony lifted up her head, her shoulders being fastened down with the strap, and prayed her uncle, by heaven, to spare her. But the relentless rod still continued to cut into her tender and now bleeding flesh, as she was told she would 'receive no mercy'.

Maud's even voice continued to number the strokes, and she herself seemed aflame; the sight of the agony her uncle was inflicting seemed to excite her sensuality in an extraordinary degree. Her lips were moist; her eyes swam; the eyelids drooped; and all the indications of a very lovesick girl appeared in her. The bleeding bottom, the tightly-strapped limbs, the piercing cries, and the relentlessly inflicted punishment excited her strongest passions. She could have torn Alice limb from limb; and she encouraged her uncle, by rolling his balls and pulling and squeezing his prick, to continue the punishment in the severest manner.

She gloated over the numbers as she called them out.

Sir Edward, too, seemed beside himself. His eyes were as two flames; he watched every motion of Alice's body; gloated upon all she displayed; could have made his teeth meet in her delicate flesh, which he lacerated with the rod yet more severely as his organ, already excited to an enormous size, was still further enlarged by Maud's hand.

At length, Alice's lower bottom having been well waled from right to left, as well as from left to right, there remained but the nine strokes to be given lengthwise.

For these, Sir Edward took the third birch from Maud, who by this time was standing with her legs wide apart, uttering little sounds and breathing little sighs of almost uncontrollable desire.

The unhappy culprit's yells had somewhat lessened, for the flowing blood had relieved the pain; and it had also been so severe that her sensitiveness to it had much diminished. But now, feeling the rod curling round her cunt, which, being all open and wet, was more than ever exposed, she yelled in a perfectly delirious manner

After some few of these strokes had been given, her uncle asking her whether he was a wretch and a monster, as she had called him last night, she replied with vehement denials.

'No! oh, no! oh! oh! oh! oh, no! Not a monster! Not a wretch! My own dear uncle, whom I love! Oh! oh! oh! My bottom burns! Oh! oh! It is on fire!'

'Will you be a good, obedient girl, miss?'

'Yes! Yes! *Yes!* Oh! indeed – '

'And thank me for whipping you?'

'Yes; indeed I do.'

'Whip well in, uncle,' said Maud quietly, in her rich voice.

And he did so. Alice shrieked; flooded the floor with urine, and fainted!

Maud, beside herself, threw herself backwards on the long and broad divan – her breasts exposed, her legs (without drawers) wide extended. Sir Edward, throwing down the birch, flung himself upon her with fury. He inserted his enormous affair into her burning cunt, and he fucked her so violently that she almost fainted from delight.

When Alice came round and Sir Edward had risen from Maud's bosom, Maud said, in clear tones: 'Uncle, I told Alice yesterday evening, when she kept me so long before I could succeed in tying her hands, that I would take care it secured her an extra half-dozen.'

'Oh, uncle! I beg Maud's pardon. Oh! after all I have gone through, let me off that half-dozen. Oh, *dear* Maud! do ask uncle to let me off. Oh, do! If I am birched any more I shall go mad! I shall – I shall indeed!'

Maud, still lying back on the couch, supported by a big, square pillow, said nothing. Her hands were clasped behind her head.

But Sir Edward said: 'No miss; you can never be let off! You must have the half-dozen. It will be a lesson to you.' And taking up the birch, he gave her six severe strokes, distributed evenly all over her bottom.

As they were being administered, Maud's left hand stole down to her waist and found its way between her legs.

While Alice was smothering her sobs and cries after her last half-dozen, Sir Edward again threw himself upon Maud and enjoyed her.

About ten minutes or a quarter of an hour later he proceeded to unstrap Alice.

She could not stand without Maud's help. The cushion and carpet were soaked with her urine and stained with her blood.

'You will tomorrow have a dozen on the trapeze, miss, for disgracing yourself in this beastly manner; you will write out fifty times, "I pee'd like a mare before my uncle"; and for the next fortnight you will only pee twice in the twenty-four hours. And now come and kiss the rod and say: "Thank you, my dear uncle, for the flogging you have given me." '

Quite docilely she knelt down before him, kissed the rod he held to her lips, and repeated the words.

'Will you be a good, obedient girl in future?'

'Yes, dear uncle; indeed I will!'

'That's a good thing. There is, you see, nothing like a good, sound flogging for a girl. Were the rod more in use what very much better women we should have. Now go with Maud and get some refreshment. I have various engagements, and shall not be in till dinner. After lunch you had better have a sleep.' And so saying, he packed the two girls off to Alice's room, shut the yellow-room door and, ringing for a footman, gave orders that the estate steward and horses should be in attendance at the front door in half an hour.

Maud and Alice went to the latter's room. By Maud's advice, Alice, who was so sore that she could scarcely move, got into bed and had some strong broth and Burgundy, and presently fell asleep. Maud spent her afternoon at an open window reclining in a lounge chair, pretending to read a novel, but in reality revelling in the reminiscences of the morning and meditating upon its delights – and wondering when she would get whipped next herself – until she was disturbed by some afternoon visitors.

CHAPTER THREE

Mystery

*'My passions, however, are very strong; but my Soul and Body
are hostile sisters, and the unhappy pair, like every imaginable
couple, lawful or unlawful, live in a perpetual state of war.'*
MADAMOISELLE DE MAUPIN

Alice's slumbers were profound. For four or five hours she continued
in the deepest sleep; but as consciousness gradually returned to her she
dreamt: and dreamt, as she had never done before, of love. Her
innocence was gone, and she would awake an experienced girl. Her
dreams were of the softest pleasures; they were prompted by that new
and wonderful sensation, under the influence of which she still was,
which had been roused once for all while she lay ignominiously
extended under her uncle's eye and received the cruel lashes of the
birch upon the most secret and divine organ of her exquisite body.
They, it is true, profaned the Temple; but they summoned to life the
Divinity there enshrined. Her sexual instincts were aroused, she
became conscious of her femininity. She felt the influence of Man, and
a longing and insatiable desire to possess him. She now knew why she
was beautiful, and in her dreams she pictured herself with soft delight –
her velvety skin, her soft, plump, round arms; her throbbing bosom,
and the ravishing sinuosities of her back – as being embraced by her
uncle; she felt his weight on the front of her thighs, she imagined his
tongue again between her lips. Her body glowed; her charms ripened;
her mind, casting away the prudish veils with which it had so long been
encumbered, already contemplated life in another and rosier light, and
prepared her to bloom into that lovely and beautiful woman she was so
soon to become.

Innocence! (so called) and virginity! in you we do not believe.
Flowers, not of virtue, but of a dunghill; the conceptions and impure
fruit of Shame, begotten upon Superstition – this is the pedigree we
give to you. Ye are fostered by those who fatten upon the fears of the

ignorant and weak-minded. Poor human creature, trembling upon the threshold of nature's holiest of holies; terror-stricken at the revelation of her most tremendous mystery about to be made you; you are swooped upon by the priest and called upon to deny your own nature! Your young and budding desires are described to you as sin, such as will condemn you hereafter to endless flame! Impurity is imputed to the most natural and the chastest passion which can possess the soul! and, outraged by the obscene imputation, it recoils in horror upon itself; but if initiated, if forearmed with knowledge, it crushes and stamps the foul tempter under foot, exclaiming: 'Monster! the obscenity is in thee. Avaunt!'

Yes; we would have it enacted that all young creatures who had not by one and twenty years of age become women should be made so by compulsory union with a lover; and as the measure could not have a retrospective effect, all old maids – incomplete human creatures, mentally and physically, that they are – should be given three months and the services gratuitously of the most energetic advertising agency in the matrimonial market, and if they did not within that period form some true union and become the fulfilment and completement of some man (for no man is perfect until he includes woman), and, moreover, produce to the court incontestable proofs of the destruction of their maidenhead, that they should perish ignominiously as unnatural deformities. And so infatuated are many of these old deformities that we believe some would perish, although no doubt most would prefer forcible violation; and therefore those who, at the end of the three months, failed to produce the required evidence in court should be given one more chance. They should be placed in charge of a robust curate or other officer of the court, and this charge should be called marriage; the union to endure during the joint lives of the parties; and if at the end of the year the husband swore that all his efforts to storm his old virgin's citadel had failed, the marriage should be declared null; the old woman transfixed by the usher with a weapon to be duly provided for the purpose, and fitted to carry it out, and then strangled; and the curate or other officer provided forthwith with another beauty.

You will say this marriage of yours is a punishment; and we reply, perhaps marriage always is, but in this case that it ought to be so, as the men concerned – all of them – should be those, and those only, who have been indicted and convicted before a court composed of young women, of not having found and enjoyed a mistress before the completion of their twenty-fifth year. We apprehend that the class would not be very numerous, and 'marriage' would therefore receive a salutary limitation.

But listen! Alice is rubbing her eyes and puzzling herself with reasons why she should be so possessed by the idea of, and longing for, her uncle, who had used her so cruelly. His being somehow or other overshadows her, and she seems to long to be absorbed in it. The strictest analysis of her craving only reduced it as far as a wish that he should take her in his arms and do with her what he wished – what that would be she knew not, but instinctively felt it would be something tremendous, which would entirely alter her whole subjective existence. He had seen her naked; he had reduced her, naked, to absolute submission to his will; he had inflicted upon her the cruellest pain; and the direct medium of the infliction of this pain had been the most secret portion of her body. Yet she delighted in the notion that *he* had seen her (with the exception solely of her stockings) completely nude; she enjoyed the idea that his hand had inflicted the stripes of which she still felt the effects; her breath came more quickly and she trembled with joy when she called to mind that it was to him she had been compelled to display, with the greatest possible humiliation to her, the most intimate recesses of her person and her most jealously concealed charms without any reserve whatsoever.

She was much puzzled, and her perplexity was accentuated as she moved and felt how tender and how sore her bottom still was.

'Shall I ever be able to sit down again?' she wondered.

Then she recollected the catastrophe that had taken place the moment before she had swooned in that inexplicable ecstasy, and her cheeks flushed and grew hot with shame. And they flushed again and grew still hotter the second time when she recollected that she had to write out fifty times, 'I pee'd like a mare before my uncle.'

What a little beast she was, and how well she deserved flogging! How just and proper it was that for the next fortnight she should be allowed to relieve herself but twice in the twenty-four hours. The inconvenience would be a very proper lesson for so naughty a girl as she was.

In the midst of these reflections, in came Maud with some egg-flip.

'I would not let them disturb you for luncheon, dear, as I am sure uncle would wish you to be fresh this evening; and, besides, you must have needed the rest dreadfully. How did you like your whipping?'

'Oh, Maud, it was dreadful! How cruelly severe uncle is.'

'I suppose it has made you hate him?'

'No; that is the strangest thing about it. Last night I thought my hatred of him could not be sufficiently intense; but I now feel that I am completely mastered by him, and find that I am glad that it is so!'

'Dear Alice, that was my own experience.'

'Has he whipped you, Maud?'

'Yes, dear; and sometimes I purposely do something in order to get myself flogged.'

'How curious! When did he whip you first?'

'Oh, long ago. I must give you a full account of it another time. Did you faint with pain?'

'No. I seemed in heaven.'

'You do not seem very much exhausted; but you had better eat this cake and egg-flip – it is better for you than tea – and let me look at that poor bottom and see what can be done for it.'

So Maud sat down upon the bed, and Alice, to her own astonishment, now nothing loth, lay on her face while Maud removed all the bedclothes from her waist downwards, and, as they chatted, gently anointed her bottom with Vinolia cream, and gave her many a pleasant sensation by the adroit use she made of her hands and fingers.

Alice explained that she now felt a much more experienced girl, and much surprised at a former coyness which she thought must have appeared extremely ridiculous.

She wondered that anyone could be prudish.

'Yes,' said Maud, 'it is want of education' – smiling – 'and as for modesty, I verily believe innocent girls are only just one little bit less nasty than the very British old maid herself,' ended Maud, with a delicious laugh. 'And you, Alice,' she went on, 'how absurd you were when first you came, blushing at every second word, buttoning your dress up to your throat, wearing it on the ground, and almost screaming at the mere mention of an ankle.'

'Oh, Maud, you do not know what I went through in the yellow room. When uncle turned up my petticoats and whipped me, and made me take off my own drawers before him – oh! oh! oh! the mere thought of it is fearful – and then when he put me across his knee and put his finger and thumb – '

'Where?' asked Maud.

'Oh, one in front and the other behind' – hiding her face with her hands

'Like that?' said Maud.

'Yes. Just like that. Oh, Maud! oh, how nice! Well, dear, the wonder is that I am alive.'

'The sweetest has to come yet, Alice dear. You said you were glad that uncle had mastered you. Do you not long for him?'

'Oh, Maud, I cannot tell you how I do. In such a strange way. I feel I could devour him!'

'Well, dear, all in good time. At any rate, you will not wish to conceal your charms now.'

'Oh, no. I take quite a healthy delight in displaying them. I think a long dress quite immodest, because it must be a sign of a mind itching with nasty thoughts. Unless, indeed,' she continued, after a moment's thoughtfulness, 'it is because the natural growth has been checked.'

'Oh, Alice, I am so glad that you are such a sensible girl. What splendid times we shall have together. I was never before so fully convinced how right uncle is in his opinion that there is nothing like a sound flogging for a girl. But although we have such a good opinion of ourselves, there are heaps of people who would condemn us with faint praise, and say we were only engagingly immoral. Uncle told me once it was because we were free and emancipated and capable of freely enjoying pleasure which the silly geese – although it is such a *natural* pleasure – think they are bound to deny themselves. There, Alice dear,' ceasing her rubbing, which she had so caressingly done; 'is the poor bottom better?'

'Yes, thank you, Maud dear, ever so much. I feel so surprised at being able to lie so unconcernedly before you.'

'You see, Alice, you are emancipated – almost. Now you had better have a warm bath, and mind that you use the soap scented with attar of roses. Make a good lather, and bathe yourself all over with it. And then, my dear, you are to put on a low chemise of black silk trimmed with yellow, a yellow corset, black silk petticoats, yellow stockings and shoes, and a net dress with great big yellow spots all over it. It won't come below your knees, dear,' said Maud, significantly, at which Alice gave a joyous laugh. 'In your bosom you are to place some yellow roses which the gardener has been ordered to bring in on purpose for you.

'And,' went on Maud, interrupting Alice, 'you are to have your hair twisted up in one great coil and fastened with this arrow, which, you see, is studded with cairngorms, and round your throat,' opening a casket on the dressing table, 'you are to put this necklace' (a magnificent one of cairngorms set in brilliants). 'By the bye, you are to tie your stockings with black, not yellow garters, and mind that the first petticoat you put on is that which is lined with yellow silk. Now mind, Alice, and do not make a mistake.'

'Oh! how lovely!' cried Alice. 'How good you are to me, you dear

Maud, to take such an interest in me. I shall be dressed all in black and yellow. Why? I wonder.'

'Because,' mockingly answered Maud, 'black and yellow are the devil's colours, and you have his beauty.'

'Now, Maud, you are laughing at me. I wonder what you will wear?'

'Oh, something not so striking, dear. You see, it is your turn tonight. You are to be the heroine of tonight. And before I go to dress, I must say goodbye to you, Alice, for I shall not have another opportunity of doing so during the evening, and tomorrow I shall not see you a girl again.'

'What on earth do you mean, Maud?' asked Alice, experiencing an unaccountable sensation of which she did not understand the significance. 'You are not going away, surely?' in alarm

'Oh, no, you dear goose,' replied Maud. 'I only meant that I should not see you a girl tomorrow because in all probability you will then be a woman,' and the room rang with the musical and merry peal of laughter Maud gave.

'You speak in riddles, dear. I wish you would explain, and not tease me so.'

'Not I,' said Maud 'Write to Miss Ada Ballin, of the *Ladies' Pictorial*, duly enclosing a coupon, and she will tell you the difference between a girl and a woman; or, by the bye, as it is not the sort of matter the editor (who ought to be circumcised) would allow an explanation of publicly, you had better send her a fee for a private reply; or, better still,' she went on maliciously, 'ask her for the address of a medical man competent to set forth the mystery personally to you, and,' said Maud, in shrieks of laughter at her own wit, 'Miss Ada Ballin will certainly send it, if you enclose a stamped, addressed envelope so that it may be sent you privately, as it would be a violation of professional etiquette to publish it; and misses are said to hate violation of every sort. Come! Come! Alice,' seeing that Alice began to pout, thinking that Maud was laughing at her, 'do not be offended at my nonsense You will know all about it by tomorrow yourself. Dear me, there's the dressing bell. Only an hour to dinner. Whoever would have thought it was so late?'

'Why not stop and dress here?'

'No; not tonight, dear. One word more, Alice. I heard that you are, for the next fortnight, only to go somewhere twice every day. Now, dear, take my advice and do it as late as you can after dinner, and in the morning after you have left the yellow room, if you have to go there. And I know you have to tomorrow.'

'Yes; I have; but I do not dread it so much. But I am not going to be birched; am I?'

'No, dear. You are going to have a dozen on the trapeze, which is in some respects worse. I can't stop to explain, though, because, if I do, I shall be late, and then I should be birched.'

'Oh, Maud! Very well, dear, I will take your advice, with thanks.'

'I am sure you will find it good. Here's Janet. I must run off.'

'What? Miss Maud in here after the bell has rung. Get off to your room, miss, or ye'll have the tawse, and nae doot aboot it.'

Then the old Scotch maid, without ado, stripped Alice stark naked and conducted her to her bath. Though she treated her like an infant, and gave her a pinch and a smack or two on the buttocks if she considered Alice was slow in obeying her directions, yet she washed and dressed her with tenderness and care, mingled with a certain amount of reverence for the girl's absolute loveliness.

'She's a bonnie bit lassie anyhow; but, gudeness guide us, what a lashing she has had about her puir body.'

She would not, however, allow any nonsense on Alice's part. The yellow corset was laced as she thought proper. Alice's protests were unheeded, and her breasts were placed in what she still considered unnecessary prominence. The roses were placed between them. The magnificent hair, done up in one great coil, was rolled up on the top of her shapely little head and fixed with the arrow, which sparkled with the brilliants in the setting of the great cairngorms. At last her toilette was complete, and, bewilderingly and bewitchingly beautiful, exciting not only her rugged Scotch attendant's admiration (who exclaimed, 'It was not work thrown away to deck so bonnie a bairn as herself') but her own, she descended to the drawing-room with that gently undulating motion which adds so greatly to the fascinations even of those who may otherwise possess charms of the highest degree.

In the drawing-room she found Maud and Sir Edward; to her surprise, there was no one else. But Sir Edward was dressed *fin de siècle*, and was gay with a yellow rose in his buttonhole. And Alice blushed with gratification when she noticed, as she did the instant she saw it, that it was precisely the same kind of rose as those in her bosom and the single one in her hair. Maud looked demurely lovely, and, though dressed in the height of fashion, had somehow good-naturedly managed to efface herself so that she might not interfere with Alice's triumph.

Then they went to dinner, Alice, again to her surprise, on her uncle's arm and at the head of the table.

'Maud has abdicated in your favour tonight, my dear, although, it is true, it is not your week. But she has only surrendered the glories to you, so do not be disturbed about the responsibilities,' her uncle added, kindly, noticing a slightly anxious expression appear.

The table groaned with summer fruits in chased gold dishes, and was decorated entirely with white roses. Never did soup taste more delicious or were its odours and flavours more appreciated; never did the chicken of the ocean, the twisted whiting or the lordly salmon or the saintly sole meet, or were they better qualified to meet, with heartier approval; never was the wine in better order – although Alice thought the Chablis (La Moutonne) a little too heavy. The champagne, iced to a nicety by the portly butler, was not on this occasion Dry Monopole, but a sweeter wine, which pleased Alice more. It soon added cordiality to a gay and merry scene. Sir Edward sent his compliments to the delighted chef upon the production by him of a work of art which had occupied that artist ever since he had received the necessary hint from Maud. It reminded her, said Alice, 'of nothing so much as of a wedding cake', at which Maud covertly smiled. It was a representation in confectionery of Venus, her cupids, her doves and her triumphs. The figure reminded Alice for a moment of her own. It was not until afterwards she discovered that in a panel of her bedroom was fixed a secret camera, and that while the night before she had stood for but a minute naked before her glass, Sir Edward had found time to take an instantaneous photograph of her, and that it was this photograph which, shown to the enraptured chef by Maud, had proved his inspiration. Sir Edward was enraptured, too, as he gazed, and the message for his cook was delivered with such warmth to his own valet that that functionary, immoveable although he appeared, was quite startled in reality. And his description of his master's earnestness pleased the genius of the kitchen quite as much as the jewel which Sir Edward had taken off his own finger and sent with the message. Monsieur Philippe felt that the ambition of a lifetime was to some extent attained, and thanked his gods that he possessed a master who could appreciate the efforts of genius.

After dinner was served that rare growth of Burgundy, Romance Conti, than which no Clos Vougeot or Chambertin or any other growth of the Côte d'Or is more delicious. Château Laffite, Château La-Rose, Château Margaux suggest, they do not equal it. And they are clarets. It is a wine which fills the veins with an elixir of life, and so Alice thought it. Why she was made so much of; why she was so petted, she could not understand. Was that courteous and gallant cavalier, opposite her at the other end of the table, not more like a lover in his addresses than her guardian, that cruel and relentless uncle who had flogged her with such merciless severity in the morning, and who was, she recollected with wonder, again to punish her on the morrow? And then she called to mind herself. Was the laughing girl, full of jokes and mirth, the beauty decked out in black and yellow, displaying with such artless coquetry her many charms, and giving herself in her high spirits so many winning airs, and feeling so much at ease, although she had no drawers on, as Maud and her uncle knew, and although her dress only barely came down to her knees, at all of which she was now rather more pleased than otherwise – the same Alice she had formerly known, dressed in a high-fitting, tight, dowdy brown garment, and expiring with shame at the sight of half an inch of leg? She laughed with joy to feel that she was becoming free from such ridiculous notions, and rejoiced at the growing sense of liberty to enjoy the possession of her charms, and to employ the power they gave her to the uttermost.

After dinner they went to a room upstairs, panelled with rose-coloured silk and hung with water-colours.

CHAPTER FOUR

Mystery Unveiled

'Away!' she cried, 'grave face and solemn sighs;
  Kiss and be merry! Preach the sermon after.
Give me the careless dance and sparkling eyes,
  Let me be wooed with kisses, songs, and laughter!'
                    THE MONKS OF THELEMA

Then up he got and donned his clothes,
  And dupped the chamber door,
Let in the maid that out a maid
  Never departed more.
                    OLD SONG: SHAKESPEARE

It was a beautiful summer's night. The air was heavily laden with the sweet perfume of the flowers in the garden below the windows, which were thrown wide open. There were besides several china vases, or rather bowls, standing about the room, full of roses, of shades varying from the deepest crimson to the softest blush scarcely more than suggested upon the delicate petal. The only sounds were the gentle rustle of the summer zephyr amongst the trees and the weird hoot of the owls. The deeply shaded lamps gave animation to the rosy tints of the boudoir. They were emphasised by the yellow flame of the fire which, notwithstanding the season, crackled merrily in the grate. (A fire upon a summer's night is an agreeable thing.) Between it and Alice there at once appeared to be something in common. She and the fire were the only two black and gold things in the rosy apartment. The fierce flame struck Alice as being a very adequate expression of the love she felt seething in her veins. She felt intoxicated with passion and desire, and capable of the most immoral deeds, the more shocking the better.

   This naughty lust was soon to have at least some gratification. Maud had seated herself at the piano – an exquisite instrument in a Louis-

Seize case – and had played softly some snatches of Schubert's airs, and Alice had been reclining some minutes on a rose-coloured couch – a beautiful spot of black and yellow, kept in countenance by the fire – showing two long yellow legs, when Sir Edward noticed that every time she altered her position she endeavoured, with a slightly tinged cheek, to pull her frock down. Of course he had been gazing at the shapely limbs and trying to avail himself of every motion, which could not fail to disclose more – the frock being very short – to view above her knee. He thought once that he had succeeded in catching a glimpse of the pink flesh above the yellow stocking.

Alice, sensible of her uncle's steadfast observation, was more and more overwhelmed with the most bewitching confusion, her coy and timid glances, her fruitless efforts to hide herself, only serving to make her the more attractive.

Maud looked on with amusement from the music-stool, where she sat pouring liquid melody from her pretty fingers, and mutely wondering whatever had come over Alice, and whatever had become of the healthy delight in displaying her charms of which she had boasted before dinner. Maud felt very curious to know how it would end.

'Alice,' at length said her uncle, with a movement of impatience, 'have you begun to write out that sentence I told you to write out fifty times?'

'Oh, no, uncle! I have not.'

'Well, my dear, you had better set to work. It will suggest wholesome reflections.'

So Alice got up and got some ruled paper, an inkstand, and a quill pen; then, seating herself at a Chippendale table, began to fiddle with the pen and ink.

Her uncle continued to watch her intently. Maud had ceased to play, and had thrown herself carelessly on the couch which Alice had just left. Maud's dress, too, was quite low and very short; but in the most artless way she flung herself backwards upon the sofa and clasped her hands behind her head, thus showing her arms, neck, bust and breast to the fullest advantage; and pulling her left foot up to her thigh, made a rest with the left knee for the right leg, which she placed across it, thus fully displaying her legs in their open-work stockings and her thighs encased in loose flesh-coloured silk drawers tied with crimson ribbons. Her attitude and abandon were not lost upon Sir Edward.

Alice's sensations were dreadful. How could she, there, under her uncle's eye, write that she had 'pee'd'? And not only 'pee'd', but with shame and anger she recollected the sentence ran, 'like a mare!' – like an animal; like a beast; as she had seen them in the street. And all 'before her uncle'. Whatever would become of her if she had to write this terrible sentence; to put so awful a confession into her own handwriting; to confide such a secret fifty times over with her own hand to paper? If it was ever found out she would be ruined – her reputation would be gone – no one would have anything to say to her – she would have to fly to the mountains and the caves. She had not realised until it came actually to writing it out how difficult, how terrible, how impossible it was for her to do it. If her uncle knew, surely he would not insist. He could not wish her to humiliate herself to such an extent; to ruin and destroy herself with her own handwriting; neither could he have realised what it would be for her to write such a thing. While these thoughts were passing through her mind, she kept unconsciously pulling and dragging at her frock. If only she could cover herself up. So much of her legs showed; and the long yellow stockings made them so conspicuous under her black frock. Although they were above her knees, unless she kept her legs close together she could not help showing her black garters. And her arms and her neck and her breast were all bare. She began to feel almost sulky.

'Well, Alice,' at length said her uncle; 'when are you going to begin?'

'Oh, uncle! it is dreadful to have to say such a thing in my own handwriting – I am sure you have never thought how dreadful.'

'You must chronicle in your own handwriting what you did, miss. Writing what you did is not so bad as doing it. And you will not only write it, but you will sign it with your name, so that everyone may know what a naughty girl you were.'

'Oh, uncle! oh, uncle! I can't. You will burn it when it is done, won't you?'

'No; certainly not. It shall be kept as a proof of how naughty you can be.' And as she kept tugging at her frock and not writing, her uncle said: 'Maud, will you fetch the dress-suspender? It will keep her dress out of her way.'

Maud discharged her errand with alacrity. In less than three minutes she had returned with a band of black silk, from which hung four long, black silk ribbons. Making Alice stand up, Maud slipped her arms under her petticoats and put the band round Alice's waist next her skin, buckling it behind, and edged it up as high as the corset, which Janet had not left loose, would allow. The four ribbons hung down far below the frock, two at the right and two at the left hip – one ribbon in front, the other at the back.

Maud then walked Alice over into the full blaze of the fire. Putting her arms round her and bending down, she took the ribbons at Alice's left side one in each hand, and then pulled them up and joined them on Alice's right shoulder in a bow. The effect, of course, was to bundle half Alice's petticoats and dress up about her waist, disclosing her left leg from the end of the stocking naked. Maud, with little ceremony, then turned her round, and, taking the ribbons at her right side, tied them across her left shoulder, thus removing the other half of Alice's covering and displaying the right leg. She then carefully arranged the frock and petticoats, smoothing them out, tightening the ribbons, and settling the bows. And by the time she had finished, from the black band round her waist nearly to her garters, Alice was in front and behind perfectly naked – her breast and arms and thighs and navel and buttocks. The lower petticoat was, it will be remembered, lined with yellow, and the inside was turned out. It and the stockings and the two black bands intensified her nakedness. She would sooner have been, she felt, stripped entirely of every shred of clothing than have had on those garments huddled about her waist, and those stockings, which, she instinctively knew, only heightened the exhibition of her form and directed the gaze to all she most wished to conceal

'Now, miss,' said her uncle, 'this will save you the trouble of vain and silly efforts to conceal yourself.'

'Oh, uncle! uncle! how can you disgrace me so?'

'Disgrace you, my dear? What nonsense! You are not deformed. You are perfectly exquisite. With,' he continued, passing his hand over her, 'a skin like satin.'

Feeling his hand, Alice experienced a delicious thrill, which her uncle noticed and recommended her to sit down and write out her imposition – a task which was now a hundred times more difficult. However could she, seated in a garb which only displayed her nakedness in the most glaring manner, write such words?

'Alice,' said he, 'you are again becoming refractory.'

Putting his arm round her, he sat down and put her face downwards across his left knee. 'You must have your bottom smacked. That will bring you to your senses.' (Smack – smack – smack – smack – smack – smack.)

'Oh, uncle! don't! Oh!' – struggling – 'I will write anything!' – smack – 'oh! how you sting!' – smack – smack – 'oh! oh! oh! Your hand is so hard.'

Then, slipping his hand between her legs, he tickled her clitoris until she cooed and declared she would take a delight in saying and writing and doing the 'most shocking things'.

'Very well, miss! Then go and write out what I told you; sign it; and bring it to me when it is finished.'

So Alice seated herself – the straw seat of the chair pricking her bottom – resolved, however, to brazen out her nakedness, and wrote with a trembling hand: 'I pee'd like a mare before my uncle; I pee'd like a mare before my uncle; I pee'd like a mare before my uncle.' Before she had half completed her task, she was so excited and to such an extent under the influence of sensual and voluptuous feelings that she could not remain still; and she felt the delicate hair in front, about her cunt, grow moist. Before she had completed the fiftieth line she was almost beside herself.

At last, for the fiftieth time, she wrote: 'I pee'd like a mare before my uncle.' And with a shudder, signed it, 'Alice Darvell'.

During her task Maud had looked at what she was writing over her shoulder, and Alice glowed with shame. So had her uncle; but Alice was surprised to find she rather liked his seeing her disgrace, and felt inclined to nestle close up to him.

Now Maud had gone to bed, and she was to take her task to her uncle.

He was seated in a great chair near the fire, looking very wide awake indeed. He might have been expected to have been dozing. But there was too lovely a girl in the room for that. He looked wide awake indeed, and there was a fierce sparkle in his eye as his beautiful ward, in her long yellow stockings and low dress, her petticoats turned up to her shoulders, and blushing deeply, approached him with her accomplished penance.

She handed it to him.

'So you did, Alice,' said he, 'so you did,' sitting bolt upright, 'pea like a mare before me, and here is, I see,' turning over a page or two, 'your own signature to the confession.'

'Oh, uncle, it is true; but do not let anyone know. I know I disgraced myself and behaved like a beast; but I am so sorry.'

'But you deserved your punishment.'

'Yes; I know I did. Only too well.'

He drew her down upon his knee, and placed his right arm round her waist, while he tickled her legs and her groin and her abdomen, and lastly her clitoris, with his hand and fingers.

He let her, when she was almost overcome by the violence of her sensations, slip down between his knees, and as she was seeking how most effectually to caress him, he directed her hands to his penis and his testicles. In a moment of frenzy she tore open his trousers, lifted his shirt, and saw the excited organ, the goal and Ultima Thule of feminine delight. He pressed down her head, and, despite the resistance she at first made, the inflamed and distended virility was very quickly placed between the burning lips of her mouth. Its taste and the transport she was in induced her to suck it violently. On her knees before her uncle, tickling, sucking, licking his penis, then looking in his face and recommencing, the sweet girl's hands again very quickly found their way to his balls.

At last, excited beyond his self-control, gazing through his half-closed lids at the splendid form of his niece at his feet – her bare back and shoulders – the breast which, sloping downwards from her position, he yet could see – her bare arms – the hands twiddling and manipulating and kneading with affection and appreciation his balls; his legs far apart, himself thrown back gasping in his armchair; his own most sensitive and highly excited organ in the dear girl's hot mouth, tickled with the tip of her dear tongue, and pinched with her dear, pretty, cruel ivory teeth – Sir Edward could contain himself no longer and, grasping Alice's head with both his hands, he pushed his weapon well into her mouth and spent down her throat. He lay back in a swoon of delight, and the girl, as wet as she could be, leant her head against his knee, almost choked by the violence of the delightful emission, and stunned by the mystery revealed to her. How she loved him! How she dandled that sweet fellow! How she fondled him! What surreptitious licks she gave him! She could have eaten her uncle.

In about twenty minutes he had recovered sufficiently to speak, and she sat with her head resting against the inside of his right leg, looking up into his face; her own legs stretched out underneath his left one – she was sitting on the floor.

'Alice, you bold, bad girl, to pee like a mare. I hope you feel punished now.'

'Oh no, uncle, it was delightful. Does it give you pleasure? I will suck you again,' taking his penis, to his great excitement, again in her warm little palm, 'if you wish.'

'My dear, do you want to pee?'

'Yes, before I go to bed.'

'Then here is the key. Run along and go to bed.'

'Oh, I would rather stay with you.'

'Although I have whipped you and birched you and smacked you and made you disgrace yourself?'

'Yes, dear uncle. It has done me good. Don't send me away.'

'Go, Alice, to bed. I will come to you there.'

'Oh, you dear uncle, how nice. Oh, do let down my things for me before I go. Some of the servants may see me.'

'And,' she continued, after an instant's pause, with a blush, and looking down, 'I want to be for you alone.'

Touched by her devotion, her uncle loosed the ribbons; let fall, as far as they would, her frock and petticoats; and giving her a kiss, and not forgetting to use his hand under her clothes in a manner which caused her again to cry out with delight, allowed her to trip off to her bedroom. But not without the remark that she had induced him to do that which did not add to her appearance; for the rich, full and well-developed girlish form bad been simply resplendent with loveliness in the garments huddled about her waist; the petticoat lining of yellow silk relieved by the black bands from her waist to her shoulder crossing each other, and bits of her black frock, with its large yellow spots, appearing here and there. And as the eye travelled downwards from the pink flesh of the swelling breasts to the smooth pink thighs, it noted with rapture that the clothes concealed only what needed not conceal-ment, and revealed with the greatest effect what did; and, still descend-ing, dwelt entranced upon the well-turned limbs, whose outlines and curves the tight stockings so clearly defined.

Sir Edward, who had made her stand facing him, and also with her back to him, was much puzzled, although so warm a devotee of the Venus Callipyge, whether he preferred the back view of her lovely legs, thighs, bottom, back, nuque and queenly little head, with its suggestion of fierce and cruel delight, or the front, showing the mount and grotto of Venus, the tender breasts, the dimpled chin and sparkling eyes, with the imaginations of soft pleasures and melting trances which the sloping and divided thighs suggested and invited.

The first thing which Alice noticed upon reaching her room was the little supper-table laid for two; and the next that there were black silk sheets on her bed. The sight of the supper – the chocolate, the tempting cakes and biscuits, the rich wines in gold mounted jugs, the Nuremburg glasses, the bonbons, the crystallised fruit, the delicate omelette – delighted her; but the black sheets had a somewhat funereal and depressing effect.

'What can Maud have been thinking of, my dear, to put *black* sheets on the bed; and tonight of all nights in the year?' asked Sir Edward, angrily, the instant he entered the apartment, and hastily returning to the sitting-room, he rang and ordered Janet up. She was directed to send Miss Maud to 'my niece's room, and in a quarter of an hour, to put *pink* silk sheets on the bed there'.

Then Sir Edward returned, and giving Alice some sparkling white wine, which with sweet biscuits she said she would like better than anything else, he helped himself to a bumper of red – standing – expecting Maud's appearance. Alice was seated in a cosy chair, toasting her toes.

Presently Maud arrived in a lovely *déshabillé*, her rich dark hair tumbling about her shoulders, the dressing-gown not at all concealing the richly-embroidered *robe de nuit* beneath it, and the two garments clinging closely to her form, setting off her lovely *svelte* figure to perfection. Her little feet were encased in low scarlet slippers embroidered with gold, so low cut as to show the whole of the white instep.

Her manner was hurried and startled, but this pretty dismay increased her attractions.

'Maud,' asked her uncle, 'what do you mean by having had black sheets put on this bed, when I distinctly said they were to be pink?'

'Indeed, indeed, uncle, you said black.'

'How dare you contradict me, miss, and so add to your offence? You have been of late very careless indeed. You shall be soundly punished. Go straight to the yellow room,' he went on to the trembling girl. 'I will follow you in a few moments and flog you in a way that you will recollect. Eighteen stripes with my riding-whip and a dozen with the cat-o'-nine-tails.'

'Oh, uncle,' she gasped.

'Go along, miss.'

Alice, to her surprise, although she had some little feeling of distress for Maud, felt quite naughty at the idea of her punishment; and, noticing her uncle's excitement, concluded instinctively that he also felt similar sensations. She was, consequently, bold enough, without rising, to stretch out her hand and to press outside his clothes the gentleman underneath with whom she had already formed so intimate an acquaintance, asking as she did so whether he was going to be very severe.

'Yes,' he replied, moving to and fro (notwithstanding which she kept her hand well pressed on him). 'I shall lash her bottom until it bleeds and she yells for mercy.'

'O, uncle!' said Alice, quivering with a strange thrill.

'Go to the room, Alice. I shall follow in a moment.'

Poor Maud was in tears, and Alice, much affected at this sight, attempted to condole with her.

'The riding-whip is terribly severe; however I shall bear it I can't tell; and then that terrible cat afterwards; it will drive me mad.'

'Oh, Maud, I am so sorry.'

'And I made no mistake. He *said* black sheets. The fact is, your beauty has infuriated him, and he wants to tear me to pieces.'

Sir Edward returned without trousers, wearing a kilt.

'Now come over here, you careless hussey,' and indicating two rings in the floor quite three feet apart, he made her stretch her legs wide, so as to place her feet near the rings, to which Alice was made to strap them by the ankles. 'I will cure you of your carelessness and inattention to orders. Your delicate flesh will feel this rod's cuts for days. Off with your dressing-gown; off with your nightdress.' Alice was dazzled by her nakedness, the ripeness of her charms, the whiteness of her skin, the plump, soft, round bottom, across which Sir Edward laid a few playful cuts, making the girl call out, for, fixed as she was, she could not struggle.

Alice then, by her uncle's direction, placed before Maud a trestle, the top of which was stuffed and covered with leather, and which reached just to her middle. Across this she was made to lie, and two rings on the other side were drawn down and fixed her elbows, so that her head was almost on the floor, and her bottom, with its skin tight, well up in the air. Her legs, of course, were well apart. The cruelty of the attitude inflamed Alice.

'Give me the whip,' said her uncle. As she handed the heavy weapon to him, he added, 'Stand close to me while I flog her, and,' slipping his hand up her petticoats on to her inflamed and moist organ, 'keep your hand upon me while I do so.'

Alice gave a little spring as he touched her. Her own animal feelings told her what was required of her.

Maud was crying softly.

'Now, miss,' as the whip cut through the air, 'it is your turn' – swish – a great red weal across the bottom and a writhe of agony – 'you careless' – swish – 'wicked' – swish – 'disobedient' – swish – 'obstinate girl.'

'Oh, uncle! oh! oh! oh! oh! I am sorry, oh, forgive – ' – swish –

'No, miss' – swish – 'no forgiveness. Black sheets, indeed' – swish – swish – swish – 'I will cure you, my beauty.'

Maud did her best to stifle her groans, but it was clear that she was almost demented with the exquisite torture the whip caused her every time it cut with relentless vigour into her bleeding flesh. Sir Edward did not spare her. The rod fell each time with unmitigated energy.

'Spare the rod and spoil you, miss. Better spoil your bold, big bottom than that,' he observed, as he pursued the punishment. The more cruel it became the greater Alice found grew her uncle's and her own excitement, until at last she scarcely knew how to contain herself. At the ninth stripe, Sir Edward crossed over to Maud's right to give the remaining nine the other way across.

Swish – swish – swish – fell the heavy whip, the victim's moans and prayers absolutely unheeded.

'A girl must have her bare bottom whipped' – swish – 'occasionally; there is nothing' – swish – 'so excellent for her' – swish – 'it teaches her to mind what is told her' – swish – 'it knocks all false shame' – swish – 'out of her; there is no mock modesty left about a young – lady after' – swish – 'she has had her bottom under the lash.'

Alice trembled when she saw the cat-of-nine-tails, made of hard, tightly twisted whip-cords, each tail bearing several knots, and when she looked at the bleeding bottom she grew sick and pale. But when her uncle began to lecture Maud as he caressingly drew the terrible scourge through his fingers, and to tell her that for a hardened girl such as she was a whip was insufficient punishment, and that she must also be subjected to the cat's claws, Alice began to revive, and she noticed that, while Sir Edward again approached boiling point, Maud gave as much lascivious movement as her tight bonds permitted.

But the first three strokes, given from left to right, evoked piercing yells and shrieks; the next three, given across the other way, cries and howls of the wildest despair, followed by low sobs. The blood flowed freely and was spattered about the room. Alice felt some on her face and arms.

'You will not forget again, I know,' said Sir Edward, as he wielded the terrible instrument. 'You careless, naughty girl, how grateful you should be to me for taking the trouble to chastise you thus. The cat has quite irresistible arguments, has she not?'

The last six were given lengthwise, first along the legs, then round the bottom, and lastly on the cunt. Maud's roars and yells were redoubled; but in an ecstasy of delight she lost her senses at the last blow.

Alice, too, was mad with excitement. Rushing off, as directed, to her room, she, as her uncle had also bid her do, tore off all her clothing and dived into the pink sheets, rolling about with the passion the sight of the whipping had stimulated to an uncontrollable degree.

Sir Edward, having summoned Janet to attend Maud, hastened to follow Alice.

Divesting himself of all his clothing, he tore the bedclothes off the naked girl, who lay on her back, inviting him to her arms, and to the embrace of which she was still ignorant, by the posture nature dictated to her, and looking against the pink sheet a perfect rose of loveliness. Sir Edward sprang upon her in a rush and surge of passion which bore him onwards with the irresistible force of a flowing sea. In a moment he, notwithstanding her cries, was between her already separated legs, clasping her to him, while he directed, with his one free hand, his inflamed and enormous penis to her virgin cunt. Already it had passed the lips and was forcing its way onwards, impelled by the reiterated plunges of Sir Edward, before Alice could realise what was happening. At last she turned a little pale, and her eyes opened wide and stared slightly in alarm, while, finding that her motion increases the assault and the slight stretching of her cunt, she remained still. But the next moment, remembering what had occurred when *it* was in her mouth, it struck her that the same throbbing and shooting and deliciously warm and wet emission might be repeated in the lower and more secret part of her body, and that if, as she hoped and prayed it might be, it was, she would expire with joy. These ideas caused a delightful tremor and a few movements of the buttocks, which increased Sir Edward's pleasure and enabled him to make some progress. But at length the swelling of his organ and his march into the interior began to hurt, and she became almost anxious to withdraw from the amorous encounter. His arms, however, held her tight. She could not get him from between her legs, and she was being pierced in the tenderest portion of her body by a man's great thing, like a horse's. Oh, how naughty she felt! And yet how it hurt! How dreadful it was that he should be able to probe her with it and detect all her sensations by means of it, while on the other hand, she was made sensible *there*, and by means of *it*, of all he felt.

'Oh! uncle! Oh! dear, dear uncle! Oh! oh! oh! oh! Wait one minute! Oh! not so hard! Oh, dear, don't push any further – oh, it is so nice; but it hurts! Oh, do stop! don't press so hard! Oh! oh! oh! Oh! please don't! oh! it hurts! Oh! I shall die! You are tearing me open! you are indeed! Oh! oh! oh!'

'If you don't' – push – push – 'hold me tight and push against me, Alice, I will – yes, that's better – flog your bottom until it bleeds and the blood runs down to your heels, you bold girl. No, you shan't get away. I will get right into you. Don't,' said he, clawing her bottom with his hands and pinching its cheeks severely, 'slip back. Push forward.'

'Oh! I shall die! Oh! oh! oh!' as she felt the pinches, and jerked forward, enabling Sir Edward to make considerable advance. 'Oh! I shall faint; I shall die! Oh, stop! Oh!' as she continued her involuntary motion upwards and downwards, 'you hurt excruciatingly.'

He folded her more closely to him, and, altogether disregarding her loud cries, proceeded to divest her of her maidenhead, telling her that if she did not fight bravely he would punish her till she thought she was being flayed alive; that he would tear her bottom for her with hooks; and he slipped a hand down behind her, and got the middle finger well into her arse.

After this, victory was assured. A few more shrieks and spasms of mingled pleasure and pain, when Sir Edward, who had forced himself up to the hymen and had made two or three shrewd thrusts at it, evoking loud gasps and cries from his lovely ward, drew a long sigh, and with a final determined push sunk down on her bosom, and she, emitting one sharp cry, found her suffering changed into a transport of delight. She clasped her uncle with frenzy to her breast, and throbbed and shook in perfect unison with him, while giving little cries of rapture and panting – with half-closed lids, from under which rolled a diamond tear or two – for the breath of which her ecstasy had robbed her.

Several moments passed, the silence interrupted only by inarticulate sounds of gratification. Sir Edward's mouth was glued to hers, and his tongue found its way between its ruby lips and sought hers. Overcoming her coyness, the lovely girl allowed him to find it, and no sooner had they touched than an electric thrill shot through her; Sir Edward's penis, which had never been removed, again began to swell; he recommenced his (and she her) upward and downward movements and again the delightful crisis occurred – this time without the intense pain Alice had at first experienced, and with very much greater appreciation of the shock, which thrilled her from head to foot and seemed to penetrate and permeate the innermost recesses of her being.

Never had she experienced, or even in her fondest moments conceived, the possibility of such transports. She had longed for the possession of her uncle; she had longed to eat him, to become absorbed in him; and she now found the appetite gratified to the fullest extent, in a manner incredibly sweet. To feel his weight upon the front of her thighs – to feel him between her legs, her legs making each of his a captive; the most secret and sensitive and essentially masculine organ of his body inside that part of hers of which she could not think without a blush; and the mutual excitement, the knowledge and consciousness each had of the other's most intimate sensations, threw her into an ecstasy. How delicious it was to be a girl; how she enjoyed the contemplation of her charms; how supremely, overpoweringly delightful it was to have a lover in her embrace to appreciate and enjoy them How delicious was love!

Sir Edward, gratified at length, rose and congratulated Alice upon her newborn womanhood, kissed her, and thanked her for the intense pleasure she had given him.

After some refreshment, as he bade her good-night, the love-sick girl once more twined her arms about him and, while slipping her legs on to the edge of the bed, she lay across it and managed to get him between them; then, drawing him down to her bosom, cried, 'Once more, dear uncle, once more before you go.'

'You naughty girl,' he answered, slightly excited; 'well, I will if you ask me.'

'Oh, please, do, uncle. Please do it again.'

'Do what again?'

'Oh! It. You know. What – what – what,' hiding her face sweetly, 'you have done to me twice already.'

'Don't you know what it is called?'

'No. I haven't the slightest idea.'

'It is called "fucking". Now, if you want it done again, you must ask to be fucked,' said he, his instrument assuming giant proportions.

'Oh, dear, I do want it ever so; but however can I ask for it . . . once more before you go?' and she lay back and extended her legs before him in the divinest fashion.

In a moment he was between them; his prick inserted; his lips again upon hers; and in a few moments more they were again simultaneously overcome by that ecstasy of supernatural exquisiteness of which unbridled passion has alone attempted to fathom the depths, and that without reaching them.

Exhausted mentally and physically by her experiences and the exercises of the evening, Alice, as she felt the lessening throbs of her uncle's engine, found she was losing herself and consciousness in drowsiness. Her uncle placed her in a comfortable posture upon the great pillow, and throwing the sheet over her, heard her murmured words of thanks and love as she fell asleep with a smile upon her face. Janet came and tucked her up comfortably. And she slept profoundly.

CHAPTER FIVE

Punishment

Whipping grown girls is a pastime rare
Few males, if called on, could refuse to share.

ROMANCE OF CHASTISEMENT

Alice lay awake next morning listening to the birds, in a sweet trance at the recollection on which she dwelt of what she had passed through the night before. She felt completely changed, and could she have seen the dark stains upon the pink sheet under her, she would have known that she really was so.

She met Maud in the breakfast-room and was warmly greeted by her.

'Well, love; well, Alice?' cried she, clasping both her hands in her own and gazing into her face with a glance in which there was deep meaning.

'Oh, Maud!' ejaculated Alice, blushing, and then, to turn the subject, 'how are you, dear, after that terrible flogging? I could almost have cried at what you suffered at one moment, and yet I could have made uncle tear you in pieces the next.'

'Yes,' said Maud; 'I have experienced the feeling. The result was that you and your uncle enjoyed yourselves the more. Now, wasn't it?'

After breakfast, Alice remembered that she had to go straight to the yellow room. She did so without much dread, feeling that she could not have worse to go through than she had already suffered; although one or two chance expressions of Maud had made her doubtful of this conclusion; and the cold sternness of her uncle startled and alarmed her after his warmth and tenderness of the preceding evening. When he met her and wished her good-morning in the breakfast-room he was apparently absolutely unconscious, and certainly totally forgetful, of what had passed.

Alice went with Maud arm-in-arm to the yellow room, wondering what the trapeze would be like.

Her uncle soon followed her and locked the door. He had a long carriage-whip and some sheets of paper which she recognised in his hand.

'You are Miss Alice Darvell, and this is your handwriting and signature?' asked he severely, showing the papers to her.

'Oh yes, uncle; they are,' answered the girl, trembling with fright.

'You pee'd like a mare before your uncle, eh, miss?'

'I – I – I couldn't help it.'

'Did you?'

'Y – ye – yes!'

'Well, you shall be flogged like a mare. Strip yourself.'

'Oh, uncle!'

'Strip yourself absolutely naked, or,' he said, raising the whip and lightly slashing it about her legs, for her frock only came down to her knees, 'you shall have double.'

She jumped as she felt the lash sting her calves, and drew up her legs one after another.

Then, seeing her uncle's arm again raised, she began quickly to undo her bodice and slip off her frock; her petticoats and corset soon followed, and, lastly, slipping off her chemise, she stood naked except for her long stockings, and covered with a most bewildering air of shame, not knowing whether to cover her face or not, or how to dispose of her hands and arms.

'Take off your shoes and stockings,' said her uncle.

She had to do so seated in her nakedness, and the action added extremely to her confusion.

Sir Edward then went to a bracket or flat piece of wood screwed on the wall, on which were two hooks fixed back to back and some distance apart; round them was fastened a thick crimson silk cord. As he unwound it, Alice saw that it communicated with a pulley in the ceiling through which it ran, and dangling from which was a bar of wood about two and a half feet long – the cord dividing about three feet above it and being fastened to each of its ends.

'Now, Maud,' said Sir Edward, 'put her in position and fix her wrists.'

Maud walked up to Alice and led her beneath the pulley. Sir Edward allowed the bar to descend to a level with the top of her shoulders. Maud then took the naked girl's right wrist and fastened it by a strap ready-prepared to one end of the bar, so that the back of the hand was against it. And then she did the same with the left hand.

'Ready?' asked Sir Edward.

'Ready,' answered Maud.

Whereupon he pulled the cord, availing himself of the hooks to get a purchase, until Alice's arms were stretched high above her head, and her whole body was well drawn up, the balls of her feet only resting on the floor.

'Oh, uncle! oh, uncle! oh, please! oh! not so high! oh! my arms will be dislocated! oh! it hurts my wrists!' and, involuntarily moving, she found very little would swing her off her feet.

Sir Edward, finding her sufficiently drawn up, fixed the cord, and, taking the whip in his right hand, played with the lash with his left as he gloated upon the exquisite naked girl – her extended arms, her shoulders, her breasts, her stomach, her navel, her abdomen, her back, her thighs, her buttocks, her legs, all displayed and glowing with shame and beauty.

At last, raising his whip, as he stood at her left, he said: 'So we "pee'd like a mare before uncle" and are now going to be flogged like a mare.'

Alice, in silent terror, drew up first one leg and then the other, showing off the exquisitely moulded limbs, and giving more than a glimpse of other charms.

'And,' went on her uncle, 'on the very part guilty of the offence.' Whisp – whisple.

He had raised the whip, swinging out the lash, and brought it down with full force across the front of the girl's thighs, the lash striking her fair on the cunt. For a moment she was speechless, but the next emitted a piercing yell as she threw her head back and struggled to be free.

Sir Edward's arm was now across him.

Whisp, whisple went the whip as he gave the return stroke severely across her bottom, making her dance with anguish and leaving a red weal.

Whisp, whisple went the whip with merciless precision back again.

Alice's gymnastics were of the most frantic description. She jumped and threw out her legs and swung to and fro, showing every atom of her form, in utter recklessness of what she showed or of what she concealed.

When three strokes had been administered backwards and forwards from the left side, Sir Edward went round to the right – there her bottom received the forward and her front the back strokes, and well laid on they were. Sir Edward delighted in the infliction of a punishment which left his victim no reserve or concealment whatever, and he made the whip cut into the flesh.

Alice, almost suffocated with her cries and sobs, writhed for several minutes after the last stroke. At last her agony became less intense and her sobs fewer.

A high stool was then put before her and on it a po.

It was pushed close up to her, and Sir Edward inserted his hand from behind and tickled and frigged her cunt, saying: 'Yesterday you pee'd to please yourself. Today you shall do so to please me.'

Alice, beside herself, knew not what to do. She had not relieved herself since the night before. At last, with a shudder, a copious flood burst out, partly over her uncle's hand, and she gave a groan as she realised the manner in which she had been made to disgrace herself.

Her uncle then loosened the rope sufficiently to let her heels rest on the ground, and calling Maud to the sofa, which was immediately in front of Alice, he threw her back on it, while she quickly unfastened and pulled down his trousers, exposing his back view entirely to Alice. Maud, too, whose petticoats were up to her waist, threw wide her legs, and Sir Edward, prostrating himself upon her, fucked her violently before Alice.

Never was Alice so conscious of her nakedness as then.

Never, apparently, did Maud enjoy the pleasure of a good fucking more than she did in the presence of that naked and tied-up girl.

And never did Sir Edward acquit himself with greater prowess.

Alice's movements, as she saw her uncle's exertions in Maud's arms, and his strong, sinewy, bare and hairy legs, and his testicles hanging down, and heard his deep breathing and Maud's gasps and sighs – began again, but this time from pleasure instead of pain. She could not, however, as she longed to, get her hands to her cunt, and could only imitate the motions of the impassioned pair before her by a sympathetic movement to and fro – which expressed, but did not assuage her desires – and by little exclamations of longing.

At length the crisis was reached, and Sir Edward sank into Maud's embrace, while Alice could see, and imagined almost that she could *hear*, the throb, throb, throb that was sending thrill after thrill through Maud, and was causing her such a transport of delight that she seemed about to faint from it.

And then he untied her, and was about to leave them, when Alice said, in a most bewitching way: 'Could you not "fuck" ' (a deep blush) 'me – just once, dear uncle?'

Her half-closed eyes, her splendid form, her nakedness, reawakened her uncle's love and reinvigorated his bestowal of those sensible proofs of it in which ladies so delight.

He replied: 'Maud has made me work pretty hard, my dear, but,' putting one hand upon her shoulder as she faced him, 'as you honour me with such a command, I should be but a *fainéant* and ungallant knight were I not to execute it – or at any rate to make an effort to do so,' and, leading the beautiful girl, nothing loth, to the couch whereon he had enjoyed Maud and gently pushing her backwards, amid her cries and exclamations and involuntary but pretty reluctance, he inserted himself into her embrace. She inundated him at once, and Maud, perceiving it, slipped her hand between his thighs. This help, good at need, soon worked the cavalier up to a proper appreciation of the situation in which he lay, and to a due expression of his sense of it; to the lady's intense gratification especially, as her forces were sufficient to enable her a second time – and this time at exactly the right instant – to

> Tumble down,
> And break her crown

and, fortunately, *not* 'come tumbling after' Jack, as Jill does in the story.

Although her uncle gave her these marks of affection, yet he did not relent in severity. She was kept without drawers the whole fortnight – a severe punishment! And the stiff white petticoats kept what skirts she had well off her legs, so that when she was seated they could not fail to be seen.

And, indeed, after the lashing on the trapeze, she was not allowed to resume that day any garments at all.

She had been given a notebook in which she was compelled to make an entry of every fault and the punishment she was to receive for it.

In her room, on that particular day, aghast at her own nakedness, and thinking herself alone, she had taken up a pair of drawers which, by accident or design, were left there – she had gone to get ready for luncheon – and put them on, when suddenly Sir Edward entered the room.

'What do you mean, miss, by putting on those things? Did I not tell you you were to remain naked the whole of today?'

'I only put them on for a moment. I felt so ashamed of being naked.'

'Take out your book and write: For being ashamed of being naked, and for disobedience to my uncle, I am to ask him to give me two dozen with the tawse across his knee after supper this evening, and I am to remain stark naked for three days.'

'Oh! oh! oh! Forgive me, dear uncle. I won't be ashamed any more. I won't disobey you any more. I won't indeed.'

But it was no use.

At luncheon she had to sit down naked. All the afternoon she had to go about so. If only she might have had one scrap of clothing on! At dinner she could not dress, and had to appear absolutely naked again; not even shoes or slippers were permitted. And that to last three days more! All the evening naked; and as she thought of it she rolled over on to the pillow of the couch and hid her face; but, notwithstanding, felt naked still.

After supper came those terrible two dozen with the tawse. The tawse is a Scotch instrument of punishment, and in special favour with Scotch ladies, who know how to lay it on soundly. It is made of a hard and seasoned piece of leather about two feet long, narrow in the handle and at the other end about four inches broad, cut into narrow strips from about six to nine inches in length.

Alice had never seen, much less felt one.

She was commanded to bring it to her uncle, and had to go for it naked – not even a fan was allowed! How could she conceal the least of her emotions? Oh, this nakedness was an awful, awful thing!

She brought it, and opened her book and knelt down and said: 'Please, uncle, give me two dozen with the tawse for being ashamed and trying to cover my nakedness, and for my disobedience.'

'Across my knee.'

'Across – your – knee.'

'Very well. Get up. Stand sideways close up to me. Now,' taking the tawse in his right hand and putting his left arm round her waist, 'lean right down, your head on the carpet, miss,' and holding her legs with his left leg, he slowly and deliberately laid on her sore bottom two dozen well-applied stripes. Then he let her go and she rolled sprawling on the carpet with pain and exhaustion.

The three days' nakedness were rigorously enforced.

They entirely overcame and quenched every spark of shame that was left about her, and she was much the more charming. Her silly simplicity, her country ignorance, were replaced by an artless coquetry and a self-possession which took away the breath and struck those in her presence with irresistible admiration.

Other punishments, too, she had to endure, some of them of a fantastic character.

The fortnight passed rapidly; but the last week, during which she was mistress, was a trying one for her. The servants scarcely heeded a baby in short frocks, with bare legs except for her long stockings, and became careless.

Many a smacking she received across her uncle's knee in the dining-room, or wherever they might happen to be, for some shortcoming; often was she sent away hungry from the table and locked up in a black hole for hours because she had not ordered this or that, or someone had done what he disapproved of. And after supper every evening, and all night if he was in the humour, she was required to be at his disposal and to give him pleasure in every form his endless ingenuity could invent.

At the end of the week, when her drawers were restored to her, she scarcely cared for them; but had not worn them long when the recollection of having been so much without them gave her the sweetest sense of shame possible.

CHAPTER SIX

The End

Quoth she, 'Before you tumbled me
You promised me to wed.'

OLD SONG

So life continued for a long while at Bosmere Hall. The summer ripened into autumn; winter followed, and then spring – when, on good authority, it is said the thoughts turn to love.

The hunting had delighted Alice, notwithstanding that she had been once or twice soundly birched by her uncle in the open air for some error of the *ménage*, and made to ride home without trousers.

She came, however, to like these punishments; but one day she thought she had seriously offended him, for he declared his intention of marrying her to his heir. She would have preferred him.

The heir and she met at a ball. He was a charming young man. Alice's bashfulness had long departed. She recognised some likeness to her uncle – she knew his wishes. She waltzed five or six times with her cousin, who was intoxicated with her beauty and her short dress, her openwork stockings with the clocks at the side, the tiny little dancing shoes, the rosy flesh, and the perfume of love in every breath she exhaled.

They went together to supper, and afterwards retired to a distant conservatory. Soon his arm was about her, while his other hand was busily engaged, to her delight, underneath her petticoats. The honeyed phrases and sweet nothings that so please lovers followed, and they were to be married in three months. The period rapidly passed.

On her wedding day her uncle presented her with a hundred thousand pounds personal property of his own, which became her own, apart from her husband and the inheritance and settlements, and also with the famous cairngorms.

Alice smiled and wept, as brides will, on her departure to spend Easter with her husband in Rome.

She taught him much, and, on the other hand, learned one or two things from him. But what surprised her most of all was that, whilst she often thought with ridicule and contempt of the days spent with her old aunt in Yorkshire, she always regarded with joy and satisfaction those spent at Bosmere Hall with her uncle and Maud, and felt she would ever consider them the happiest of her life.

'The most secret parts of virgins have been submitted to the examination of ignorant matrons and prejudiced physicians, without dreaming that such an act of indecency is an offence against virginity; that the attempt to discover it is a rape in itself; that every shameful situation and every indecent condition at which a virgin is obliged to blush within, is a real defloration.'

BUFFON

Wordsworth Classic Erotica

❧ ⚜ ❧

ANONYMOUS
*The Autobiography
of a Flea*

Blue Velvet

Eveline

Frank and I

First Training

A Night in a Moorish Harem

The Pearl

Randiana

The Romance of Lust

Sadopaideia

Suburban Souls

Teleny

GUILLAUME APOLLINAIRE
*The Amorous Exploits of
a Young Rakehell*

GIOVANNI BOCCACCIO
*Selections from
The Decameron*

JOHN CLELAND
*Memoirs of a Woman of
Pleasure – Fanny Hill*

SHEIKH NEFZAOUI
The Perfumed Garden
TRANSLATED BY
SIR RICHARD BURTON

PAULINE REAGE
The Story of O

EDWARD SELLON
The New Epicurean

SMITHERS AND BURTON
Priapaia

ALGERNON CHARLES
SWINBURNE
The Whippingham Papers

VARIOUS
*The Olympia Reader –
Volume One*

*The Olympia Reader –
Volume Two*

VATSYAYANA
The Kama Sutra

'WALTER'
My Secret Life – Volume One
My Secret Life – Volume Two

LI YU
The Carnal Prayer Mat